A Thoughtl

Helen H. Gardener

Alpha Editions

This edition published in 2023

ISBN : 9789357948463

Design and Setting By
Alpha Editions
www.alphaedis.com
Email - info@alphaedis.com

PREFACE TO THE EIGHTH EDITION.

In issuing a new edition of this book, it has been thought wise to state that an unauthorized edition is now on the market, and it is desirable that the public shall know that all copies of this book not bearing the imprint of the Commonwealth Company are sold against the will and in violation of the rights of the author.

Since some persons have been puzzled to make the connection between the title of the book and the stories themselves, and to apply Colonel Ingersoll's exquisite autograph sentiment more clearly, a part of "An Open Letter," which was written in reply to an editorial review of the book when it first appeared, is here reprinted, in the hope that it may remove the difficulty for all.

AN OPEN LETTER.

I have, this morning, read your review of "A Thoughtless Yes." I wish to thank you for the pleasant things said and also to make the connection—which I am surprised to see did not present itself to your mind—between the title and the burden of the stories or sketches.

It is not so easy as you may suppose to get a title which shall be exactly and fully descriptive of a collection of tales or sketches, each one of which was written to suggest thoughts and questions on some particular topic or topics to which people usually pay the tribute of a thoughtless yes. With one—possibly two—exceptions each sketch means to suggest to the reader that there may be a very large question mark put after many of the social, religious, economic, medical, journalistic, or legal fiats of the present civilization.

You say that "in 'The Lady of the Club' she [meaning me] does not show how poverty results from a thoughtless yes. Perhaps she does not see that it does." I had in my mind exactly that point when I wrote the story and when I decided upon the title for the book. No, I do not attempt in such sketches to show *how*, but to show *that*, such and such conditions exist and that it is wrong. I want to suggest a question of the justice and the right of several things; but I want to leave each person free to think out, not my conclusion or remedy, but a conclusion and a remedy, and at all events to make him refuse, henceforth, the thoughtless yes of timid acquiescence to things as they are simply because they are. In the "Lady of the Club" I meant to attack the impudent authority that makes such a condition of poverty possible, by calling sympathetic attention to its workings. There are one or two other ideas sustained by authority, to which, to the readers of that tale, I wished to make a thoughtless yes henceforth impossible. At least I hoped to arouse a question. One is taxation of church property. I wished to point out that by shirking their honest debts churches heap still farther poverty and burden upon the poor. I hoped, too, to suggest that the idea of "charity," to which most people give a warmly thoughtless yes, must be an indignity or impossibility where, even they would say, it was most needed. I wanted to call attention to the fact that a physician and a man of tender heart and lofty soul were compelled to make themselves criminals, before the law, to even be kind to the dead. That conditions are so savage under the present system that such a case is absolutely hopeless while the victims live and outrageous after they are dead. To all of these dictates of impudent authority, to which most story readers pay the tribute of a thoughtless yes, I wanted to call attention in such a way that henceforth a question must arise in their minds. I hoped to show, too, that even so lofty a character as Roland Barker was tied hand and foot—until it made him almost a madman—by a system of economics and religion and law which so interlace as to sustain each other and combine to not only crush the poor but to prevent the rich from helping along even where they desire to do so.

These were the main points upon which that particular tale was intended to arouse a mental attitude of thoughtful protest There are other, minor ones, which I need not trouble you to recall. If you will notice, nearly all of the tales end (or stop without an end) with an open question for the reader to settle—to settle his way, not mine. Indeed, I am not yet convinced that my own ideas of the changes needed and the way to bring them about are infallible. I am still open to conviction. I have tried to grasp the Socialist, Communist, Anarchist, Single-tax, Free-land, and other ideas and to comprehend just what each could be fairly expected to accomplish if established—to see the *pros* and *cons* of these and other schemes for social improvement. These, and the varying cults ranged between, each seems to me to have certain strong points and certain weak ones. Each seems to me to overlook some essential feature; and yet I have no system to offer that I think would be better or would work better than some of these. Indeed, I do most earnestly believe that *the* inspired way is yet to be struck out, and I do not believe that I am the one to do it Meanwhile I can do some things. I can suggest questions, and, sometimes, answers. But I am not a god, and I do not want all people to answer my way. I do want to help prevent, now and henceforth, the tribute of a thoughtless yes from being given to a good many established wrongs.

Since such able thinkers as you are have—in the main—already refused such tribute, I am perfectly satisfied to let each of these answer the questions I have suggested or may suggest in my fiction in the way that seems most hopeful to him.

Meantime, the vast majority of story readers have not yet had their emotions touched by the dramatic presentation of "the other side." Fiction has—in the main—worked to make them accept without question all things as authority has presented them. Who knows but that a lofty discontent may be stirred in some soul who can solve the awful problems and at the same time reconcile the various cults of warring philosophers so that they may combine for humanity and cease to divide for revenue—or personal pique? I do not believe that the province of a story is to assume to give the solution of philosophical questions that have puzzled and proved too much for the best and ablest brains. I have no doubt that fiction may stir and arouse to thought many who cannot understand and will not heed essays or argument or preaching, while it may also present the same thoughts in a new light to those who do. Personally I do not believe in tacking on to fiction a "moral" or an "in conclusion" which shall switch all such aroused thoughts into one channel. Clear thinking and right feeling may lead some one, who is new to such protest, to solutions that I have not reached. So let us each question "impudent authority," whether it be in its stupid blindness to heredity or to environment; and I shall be content that you solve the new order by an appeal to Anarchism *via* free land; or that Matilda Joslyn Gage solve it by the ballot for women and hereditary freedom from slavish instincts stamped upon a race born of superstitious and subject mothers.

Personally I do not believe that all the free land, free money or freedom in the world, which shall leave the mothers of the race (whether in or out of marriage) a subject class or in a position to transmit to their children the vices or weaknesses of a dominated dependent, will ever succeed in populating the world with self-reliant, self-respecting, honorable and capable people.

On the other hand, I do not see how the ballot in the hands of woman will do for her all that many believe it will. That it is her right and would go far is clear; but after that, your question of economics touches her in a way that it does not and cannot touch men, and I am free to confess that as yet I have heard of no economic or social plan that would not of necessity, in my opinion, bear heaviest upon those who are mothers. So you will see that when I suggested the desirability in "For the Prosecution" of having mothers on the bench and as jurors where a case touched points no man living does or can understand in all its phases, I do not think that would right all the wrong nor solve all the questions suggested by such a trial; but I thought it would help push the car of right and justice in the direction of light which we all hope is ahead.

You believe more in environment than in heredity; I believe in both, and that both are sadly and awfully awry, largely because too many people in too many ways pay to impudent authority the tribute of a thoughtless yes.

It is one of the saddest things in this world to see the brave and earnest men who fight so nobly for better and fairer economic conditions for "Labor," pay, much too often, the tribute of a thoughtless yes to the absolute pauper status of all womanhood They resent with spirit the idea that men should labor for a mere subsistence and always be dependent upon and at the financial mercy of the rich. They do not appear to see that to one-half of the race even that much economic independence would be a tremendous improvement upon her present status. How would Singletax or Free-land help this? You may reply that Anarchism would solve that problem. Would it? With maternity and physical disabilities in the scale? To my mind, all the various economic schemes yet put forward lack an essential feature. They provide for a free and better manhood, but they pay the tribute of a thoughtless yes to impudent authority in the case of womanhood, in many things. And so long as motherhood is serfhood, just so long will this world be populated with a race easy to subjugate, weak to resist oppression, criminal in its instincts of cruelty toward those in its power, and humble and subservient toward authority and domination. Character rises but little above its source. The mother molds the man. If she have the status, the instincts, and the spirit of a subordinate, she will transmit these, and the more enlightened she is the surer is this, because of her consciousness of her own degradation.

Look at the Kemmler horror. People all marvel at his "brutish nature and his desire to kill." No one says anything about the fact, which was merely mentioned at his trial, that his "father was a butcher and his mother helped in the business." Did you know that this is also true of Jesse Pomeroy; the boy who "from infancy tortured animals and killed whatever he could?"

Would all this sort of thing mean absolutely nothing to women of the same social and scientific status enjoyed by the men who assisted at the trials of these two and at the legal murder of one? In ordinary women, of course, it would not stir very deep thought But these were not ordinary men. They were far more than that, Almost all the women who have spoken or written to me of the Kemmler horror have touched that thought Have you heard a man discuss it? Is there a reason for this? Do we pay the tribute of a thoughtless yes to all that clusters about the present ideas on such subjects and about their criminal medicolegal aspects? But this letter grows too long.

With great respect and hearty good wishes,

I am sincerely,

Helen H. Gardener.

A SPLENDID JUDGE OF A WOMAN.

"We look at the one little woman's face we lovey as we look at the face of our mother earth, and see all sorts of answers to our own yearnings."—George Eliot.

"But after all it is not fair to blame her as you do, Cuthbert. She is what she must be. It is not at all strange. Midge—"

"I am quite out of patience with you, Nora;" exclaimed Cuthbert Wagner, vehemently. "How can you excuse her? Midge, as you call her, has been no friend to you. She was deceitful and designing all along. She even tried in every way she could think of to undermine you in *my* affections!" He tossed his head contemptuously and strode to the window where he stood glaring out into the moonlight in fierce and indignant protest. His wife had so often spoken well of Margaret Mintem. She did not appear to hold the least resentment toward the school-friend of her past years, while Cuthbert could see nothing whatever that was good or deserving of praise in the character of the young lady in question. He was bitterly resentful because Margaret Mintem had spoken ill of his wife while she was only his betrothed, and Cuthbert Wagner did not forgive easily.

Nora crossed the room with her swift, graceful tread, and the sweep of her lace gown over the thick rug had not reached her husband's ear as he stood thumping on the window pane. He started a little, therefore, when a soft hand was laid upon his arm and a softer face pressed itself close to his shoulder.

"It is very sweet of you, dear," she said in her low, gentle voice, "It is very sweet of you to feel so keenly any thrust made at me; but darling, you are unfair to Midge, poor girl! My heart used often to bleed for her. It must be terribly hard for her to fight her own nature, as she does,—as she *must*,—and lose the battle so often after all."

"Fight fiddle-sticks!" said Cuthbert, and then went on grumbling in inarticulate sounds, at which his wife laughed out merrily.

"Oh, boo, boo, boo," she said, pretending to imitate his unuttered words.

"I don't believe a word of it. *I know Margaret Mintem.* Did I not room with her for three long years? And do I not know that she is a good girl, and a very noble one, too, in spite of her little weakness of envy or jealousy?

"She can't help that. I am sure she must be terribly humiliated by it. Indeed, indeed, dear, I know that she is; but she cannot master it. It is a part of her. I do not know whether she was bom with it or not; but I do know that all of her life since she was a very little girl she has been so situated that just that particular defect in her character is the inevitable result. Don't you believe, Cuthbert, that all such things are natural productions? Why, dearie, it seems to me that you might as reasonably feel angry with me because my hair is brown as toward Midge because her envy sometimes overbears her better qualities. The real fault lies—"

"O Nora, suppose you take the stump! Lecture on 'Whatever is is right,' and have done with it."

"Aha, my dear," laughed his wife, "I have caught you napping again. I do not say that it is right; but I do say that it is natural for Margaret to be just what she is. That is just the point people always overlook, it seems to me. Nature is wrong about half of the time—even inanimate nature. Just look over there! See those splendid mountains and the lovely little valley all touched with moonlight; but, oh, how the eye longs for water! A lake, a splendid river, the ocean in the distance—something that is water—*anything* that is water! But no, it is valley and mountain and mountain and valley, until the most beautiful spot in the world, when first you see it, grows hateful and tiresome and lacking in the most important feature."

Cuthbert laughed. "A lake would look well just over there by McGuire's barn, now, wouldn't it? And, come to think of it, how a few mountains would improve things over at Newport or Long Beach." He stopped to thump a bug from his wife's shoulder.

"How pretty you look in that black lace, little woman. I don't believe nature needed any improver once in her life anyhow—when she made you."

Nora smiled. A pleased, gratified little dimple made itself visible at one corner of her mouth. Her husband stooped over and kissed it lightly, just as the portiere was drawn aside and a guest announced by James, the immaculate butler.

"We've just been having a quarrel, Bailey," said Mr. Wagner, as he advanced to greet the visitor, "and now I mean to leave it to you if—"

"Yes," drawled Mr. Bailey, "I noticed that as I came in. You were just punctuating your quarrel as James drew back the portiere. That is the reason I coughed so violently as I stepped inside. Don't be alarmed about my health. It isn't consumption. It is only assumption, I do assure you. I assumed that you assumed that you were alone—that there wasn't an interested spectator; but, great Scott! Bert, I don't blame you, so don't apologize;" and with a low bow of admiration to his friend's wife, he joined in the laugh.

"But what was the row? I'm consumed to hear it," he added, as they were seated. "I should be charmed to umpire the matter—so long as it ended that way. Now, go on; but I want to give you fair warning, old man, that I am on

Mrs. Wagner's side to start with, so you fire off your biggest guns and don't attempt to roll any twisted balls."

"*Curved* balls," laughed Nora, "not twisted; and it seems to me you mixed your games just a wee bit. There isn't any game with guns and balls both, is there?"

"Oh, yes, yes indeed," replied Mr. Bailey, promptly. "The old, old game in which there is brought to bear a battery of eyes."

"Oh, don't," said Cuthbert. "I am not equal to it! But after all, I can't see that you are well out of this, Ned. Where do the balls come in?"

"What have you against eyeballs that roll in a fine frenzy when a battery of handsome eyes is trained upon a bashful fellow like me?" he asked quite gravely, and then all three laughed and Cuthbert pretended to faint.

"I shall really have to protest, myself, if you go any farther, Mr. Bailey," said Nora.

"You are getting into deep water, and if you are to be on my side in the coming contest, I want you to have a cool head and—"

"A clean heart;" put in Cuthbert.

"Mrs. Wagner never asks for impossibilities, I am sure," said Mr. Bailey, dryly.

"But she does. That is just it. She wants to make me believe that a girl who traduced her and acted like a little fiend generally, is an adorable creature—a natural production which couldn't help itself—had to behave that way. We—"

"I believe I started in by saying that I should be on your side, Mrs. Wagner," said their guest, assuming a judicial attitude and bracing himself behind an imaginary pile of accumulated evidence, "but I'm beginning to wobble already. If Bert makes another home run like that, I warn you, madam, that while I shall endeavor to be a fair and impartial judge, I shall decide against you."

Nora's eyes had a twinkle in their depths for an instant, but her face had grown grave.

"Wait. Let me tell you." she said. "Even Cuthbert does not know just how it was—what went to make my old school-friend's character precisely what it became. It was like this: When she was a very little girl her father died, and the poor little mother went back home with her four young children, and her crushed pride, to be an additional burden to the already overburdened father, who was growing old and who had small children of his own still to educate and pilot through society. He had lost his hold on business when he went into the army; and although he came home a general, quite covered with glory, a large family cannot live on glory, you know, and fame will not buy party dresses for three daughters and a grandchild."

"I've noticed that," remarked Mr. Bailey, dryly.

"The added importance of his position and the consequent publicity made the handsome party gowns all the more necessary, however," said Nora, not heeding the interruption, "and so the family had to do a great many things that were not pleasant to make even one end meet, as poor Midge used to say. The General loved brains and his granddaughter was very bright."

Cuthbert gave a low whistle. He would not compromise. If he found one thing wrong in an acquaintance all things were wrong. It followed, therefore, in his mind, that since Margaret Min-tern had been guilty of envy, she was altogether unlikely to possess fine mental capabilities. He would not even allow that she was stylish and sang well.

His wife took no notice of his outburst, but her color deepened a little as she went on.

"She was the most clever girl mentally that I have ever known and she was a vast deal of service to me in the years we were together. She sharpened my wits and stimulated my thoughts in a thousand ways, for which I am her debtor still. But I am getting ahead of my story. As I say, the old General worshipped brains, but he also adored beauty; and, alas, his granddaughter was quite plain—"

"Ugly as a hedge-fence, and I never could see that she was so superhumanly brilliant or stylish, as you claim, either," put in Cuthbert Wagner, as he leaned back in his deep chair with his eyes drawn to a narrow line.

"She was almost exactly the same age of her Aunt Julia, the General's youngest daughter; but Julia was a dream of beauty and of stupidity."

"Situation is now quite plain," said Mr. Bailey. "The lovely Julie got there. She always does, and—"

"Ah, but you must remember that in this case 'there' was the heart of the father of one and the grandfather of the other," said Nora, smiling.

Her husband laughed outright and faced Mr. Bailey.

"I rather think she has got you now, old man. In a case like that I'm hanged if I know how it would turn out—who would get there. The elements won't mix. It is not the usual thing.

"The beautiful stupid and the brilliant but plain are all right,—regular stage properties, so to speak,—but the grandfather! I'll wager if we tossed up for it, and you got heads and I got tails we'd both be wrong.

"There is something actually uncanny in the aged grandparent ingredient in a conundrum like that. Now if it were a young fellow,—only the average donkey,—why of course the lovely Julia would bear off the palm and leave Midge, as Nora calls her, to pine away. But if it were a level-headed, middle-aged chap like me, brains would take precedence." He waved his hand lightly toward his wife, who parted her lips over a set of little white teeth and a radiant smile burst forth.

"You are a bold hypocrite, Bert," said Mr. Bailey. "You did not have to make any such choice, and you are not entitled to the least credit in the premises. You got both."

"This is really quite overwhelming," laughed Nora; "but—"

"Why on earth did you call her attention to it, Ned," exclaimed Mr. Wagner, with great pretence of annoyance. "She would have swallowed it whole. I wonder why it is a woman so loves to be told that you married her for her intellect, when in nine hundred and ninety-nine cases out of eight hundred and forty you did nothing of the kind, and she knows it perfectly well. You married her because you loved her, brains or no brains, beauty or no beauty, and that's an end of it. Isn't that so, Ned?"

"Well, I'm not prepared to say, yet. I am umpire. I have not made up my mind which I shall marry—the lovely Julia, or the brilliant niece; but I think I shall in the long run."

"God help you if you do!" said Cuthbert, dramatically. "I don't know Julia, the beautiful; but I'd hate to see you married to a cat with uncut claws, Ned, much as I think you need dressing down from time to time."

"Mrs. Wagner," said Mr. Bailey, turning to her, gravely, "I'm not paying the least attention to him, and I am eager to hear how the grandfather got out of it."

"The *grandfather!*" exclaimed Nora, "why I had no idea of telling his story. It was the two girls I was interested in——or at least, in one of them; but that is just like a man. He—"

She allowed her feather fan to fall in her lap and looked up helplessly. "But come to think of the other side, his story *would* be worth telling, wouldn't it? It must have been a rather trying situation for him, too."

She took the fan up again, and waved it before her, thoughtfully. "I wonder why I never thought of that before. I have always rather blamed him for developing his granddaughter's one sad defect. I thought he should have guarded her against it. And—I do wonder if it is because I am a woman that I never before thought how very difficult it must have been for him?"

"No doubt, no doubt," said her husband, dryly. "But now that we have shed a few tears over our mental shortcomings and lack of breadth of sympathy in overlooking the sad predicament of the doughty General, proceed. The umpire sleepeth apace, and I've got to have my shy at the charming Midge before we've done with her," and he shut his paper-knife with a wicked little click.

"You can see how it would be," Nora began again, quite gravely, and the gentlemen both smiled. "You can see how it would be. The granddaughter was made to feel that she was in the way—was a burden. Her mother would urge her to become indispensable to the old General. To read to him, talk brightly to him, sing and play for him, watch his moods and meet them cleverly. It was all done as a race for his affections. Julia raced with her, setting her beauty and the other great fact that she was the child of his old age over against the entertaining qualities of her rival."

Mr. Bailey drew his handkerchief across his brow and looked helplessly perplexed, while Cuthbert responded with a dreary shake of the head.

"It is a clear case of 'The Lady or the Tiger,' yet, so far as I can see," said he. "Who got there, Bailey?"

Mr. Bailey smiled despairingly, and shook his head, but said nothing.

"It went on like that day after day, week after week, month after month, year after year," continued Nora, looking steadily in front of her and shivering a little, "until they were both young ladies. The General gave a party to present them both to society at the same time. His granddaughter tried to make him feel that he was repaid for the expense and trouble by the display of her exceptional powers as a conversationalist—Julia, by the display of her neck and shoulders, her exquisite rose-leaf face, and her childishly pretty manners. This sort of rivalry would have been well enough, no doubt, if it had not been for the fact that from childhood up to this culmination there had been a dash of bitterness in it, an un-der-current of antagonism; and poor Midge had always been the main sufferer, because she was very sensitive and she was made to feel that all she received was taken from her aunt Julia. To stand first with her father, Julia would do almost anything; and the ingenuity with which she devised cruel little stabs at Midge was simply phenomenal. To be absolutely necessary to him became almost a mania with his granddaughter."

"If this thing goes on much longer, I am going to have a fit," Cuthbert announced, placidly.

"The girl you judge so harshly, poor child, had a great many of them," said Nora, with an inflection in her voice that checked a laugh on Mr. Bailey's lips. "Fits of depression, fits of anger, fits of sorrow, fits of shame and of indignation with herself and with others. For there were times when she stooped to little meannesses which her sensitive soul abhorred. If intense effort resulted, after all, in failure, envy of her successful rival grew up in her heart; and, sometimes, if it were carefully cultivated by the pruning hook of sarcasm or an unkind look of triumph, she would say or do a mean or underhand thing, and then regret it passionately when it was too late."

Cuthbert gave a grunt of utter incredulity.

"Regretted it so little she'd do it again next day," he grumbled. Nora went steadily on.

"It grew to be the one spring and impulse of her whole nature—the necessity of her existence—to stand *first* with the ruling spirit wherever she was, whoever it might be. At school I have known her to sit up all night to make sure that she would be letter-perfect in her lessons the following morning. Not because she cared for her studies so much as because she *must* feel that she stood first in the estimation of her teachers. And then, too, her grandfather would know and be proud of her. It got to be nature with her (I do not know how much of the tendency may have been born in her) to need to stand on the top wherever she was. (It has always seemed to me that the conditions surrounding her were quite enough to explain this characteristic without an appeal to a possible heredity of which I can know nothing.) Even where we boarded, although she disliked the women and looked down upon the young men, she made them all like her, and even went the length of allowing one young fellow to ask her to marry him simply because she saw that he was interested in me."

"Humph! She—" began Cuthbert, but his wife held up her hand to check him, and did not pause in her story.

"Up to that time she had not given him a thought, and she was very angry when he finally asked the great question. She thought that he should have known that such a girl as she was could not be for a man of his limitations. She felt insulted. She flew up stairs and cried with indignation. 'The mere idea!' she said to me. 'How dared he! The common little biped!' I told her that she had encouraged him, and had brought unnecessary pain upon him as well as regret upon herself. Then she was angry with me. By and by she put her hand out in the darkness and took mine and pressed it. Then she said, 'Nora, it *was* my fault; but—but—' and then she began to sob again. 'But, Nora, I don't—know—why—I—did—it—and,' there was a long pause. 'And, beside, I *thought* he was in love with you,'" she sobbed out.

"That was the whole story," said Cuthbert, resentfully. "She simply wanted to supplant you and—"

"Yes, that *was* the whole story, as you say, dear," said his wife, gently; "but the poor girl could not help it. And—and she did not understand it herself at all."

"You make me provoked, Nora," said Cuthbert, almost sharply. "She wasn't a fool. She tried the same game on me a year or two later; but that time it didn't work. She even went the length of talking ill of you to me—saying little cutting things—when she found I had utterly succumbed to your attractions. I have to laugh yet when I think of it,—that is, when it don't make me too angry to laugh,—how I gave her a good round talking to." He laughed now at the recollection.

"She must have taken me for her delightful old grandparent the way I lectured her. But when I remembered how loyal you were to her, it just made my blood boil and I told her so."

Mr. Bailey shifted his position and began to contemplate giving a verdict emphatically against the absent lady, when Nora checked him by a wave of her fan.

"Yes, I know she did, Cuthbert, and I know everything you said to her. You were very cruel—if you had understood, as you did not and do not yet. She came and told me all about it." Cuthbert Wagner gave a low, incredulous whistle, and even Mr. Bailey looked sceptical.

"She came back from that drive with you the most wretched girl you ever saw. Her humiliation was pitiful to see. Her self-reproach was touching and real. I believe she would have killed herself if I had seemed to blame her."

Cuthbert snapped out:

"Humph! Very likely; and gone and done the same thing again the next day."

"Possibly that is true—if there had been a next day with a new temptation that was too strong for her on the shore where she landed after death If—"

"If the Almighty had shown a preference for some one else, hey?" asked Mr. Bailey, flippantly.

"No doubt, no doubt," acquiesced Nora. "But suppose you had a weak leg and it gave way at a critical moment—say just when you were entering an opera box to greet a lady. Suppose it dropped you in a ridiculous or humiliating manner. You would rage and be distressed, and make up your mind not to let it occur again, except in the seclusion of your own apartments; but—well, it would be quite as likely to serve you the same trick the following week, in church."

"The illustration does not strike me as quite fair," said Mr. Bailey, judicially.

"Good, Ned! Don't let her argue you into an interest in that little cat. She was simply a malicious little—"

"Wait, then," said Nora, ignoring her husband's outburst and looking steadily at Margaret Mintem's new judge, who was showing signs of passing a sentence no less severe than if it were delivered by Cuthbert Wagner himself.

"Suppose we take your memory. Are there not some names or dates that *will* drop out at times and leave you awkwardly in the lurch?"

"Well, rather," said Mr. Bailey, disgustedly. This was his weak spot.

"Now, don't you see that a person who has a perfect memory might be as unfair to you as you are to my old school friend in her little moral weakness— if we may call it by so harsh a term as that? That was her one vulnerable spot. It may have been born in her. That I do not know; but I insist that it *was* trained and drilled into her as much as her arithmetic or her catechism were, and with a result as inevitable. She loathed her fault, but it was too strong for her. Her resolution to conquer it dropped just short of success very often, indeed; and oh! how it did hurt her when she realized it and thought it all over, for her motives were unusually pure, and her moral sense was really very high indeed."

"Moral sense was a little frayed at the edges, I think."

"Don't, Cuthbert. You are such a cruelly severe judge. I know Mr. Bailey is on my side, now, and will think you very unfair. He does not mean to be, I assure you, Mr. Bailey, and if she had not spoken ill of me he would see the case fairly. But what *are* you thinking?"

"That it is a rather big question. That I—that I have overstayed my time. I just came over to ask you to dine with us next Thursday. My mother has some friends and wants you to meet them. May I leave my judicial decision open until then?"

"Certainly. Pray over it," said Cuthbert, rising; "and if you don't come out on my side, openly,—as I know you are in your mind,—buy a wire mask. I won't have any dodging."

"Come early. There is a secret to tell," laughed Mr. Bailey as he withdrew, and then he blushed furiously. "Mother's secret," he added, as he closed the door behind him.

The evening of the dinner the Wagners were later than they had intended to be, and Mrs. Bailey took Nora aside and said quite abruptly:

"I've got to pop it at you rather suddenly. Why didn't you come earlier? The lady whom Ned is to marry is here, and it is for her I have given the dinner. Ned went to your house to tell you last week, but his heart failed him. He said you were all in such a gale of nonsense that he concluded to wait. It is a very tender subject with him, I assure you. His case is quite hopeless. He is madly in love, and I am very much pleased with his choice. She seems as nearly perfect as they ever are, and she is unusually talented. But here is Ned now. I have told her all about it, my son, come and be congratulated."

He came forward shyly enough for a man of his years and experience, and took Nora's hand in a helpless way. But Cuthbert relieved matters at once by a hearty "Well, it is splendid, old fellow. I'm delighted. I—"

"But before the others come down," broke in Mr. Bailey, as if to get away from the subject, "I want to get my discharge papers in that case you plead before me last week. It lies heavy on my soul, for I am very sorry to say, Mrs. Wagner, that I am compelled to give judgment against you and your client. I think she was—I'm with Cuthbert this time. She impresses me as almost without redeeming qualities. I do not wish to make her acquaintance. I am sure that I could never force myself to take even a passing interest in that sort of a moral acrobat. Really, the lovely but selfish Julia would be my choice in a team of vicious little pacers like that. I'm sure I should detect your friend's fatal weakness in her every action. I should be unable to see anything but the hideous green-eyed monster even in the folds of her lace gowns or the coils of her shining hair. He would appear to me, ghost-like, peering over her shoulder in the midst of her most fascinating conversation. I should feel his fangs and see the glitter of his wicked eyes while I tried to say small nothings to her, and—"

"Oh, not at all," protested Nora. "You would never detect it at all unless she happened to be fighting for your esteem or admiration where she felt that odds were against her. She—"

"I beg your pardon, Mrs. Wagner, but I am quite sure that I should. Envy is to me the very worst trait in the human character. I could more easily excuse or be blinded to anything else. I *know* that I should detect it at once. I always do—especially in a woman."

"Certainly. Anybody could. You know very well, Nora, that I saw—" began Cuthbert quite gleefully; but as a salve to her wounded feelings Mr. Bailey added in a tone of conciliation to Nora:

"However, I shall agree to let you test me some day. Present your friend to me, *incog.*, and I'll wager—oh, *anything* that I shall read her like a book on sight. I'm a splendid judge of a woman. Always was from childhood. I'm sure that I should feel creepy the moment I saw the brilliant but envious granddaughter of the unfortunate old warrior. And by the way, *he* continues to be the one for whom you have enlisted my sympathy. I wonder that he was able to live two weeks in the same house with such a—"

"Cat," said Cuthbert, with a vicious jab at a paper-weight which represented a solemn-looking Chinese god in brocade trousers. He was just turning to enter into a cheerful and elaborate statement of his side of the controversy, as Mrs. Bailey swept down the room with her son's betrothed upon her arm, smiling and happy.

"Margaret Mintern!" exclaimed Nora, in dismay, and then—

"I am so glad to see you again, dear, and to be able to congratulate you, instead of some fair unknown, upon the fact that you are to have so dear a friend of ours for a husband. We think everything of Mr. Bailey. He is Bert's best friend and—"

Cuthbert had turned half away in utter confusion when he saw the ladies coming down the room, and feigned an absorption in the rotund Chinese deity which he had never displayed for the one of his own nation. But he bowed now, and mumbled some inarticulate sounds as he looked, not at the future Mrs. Bailey, but at the ridiculously happy face of her lover, whose usually ready tongue was silent as he hung upon the lightest tone of the brilliant woman beside him. As they passed into the dining-room, Nora managed to say to her husband:

"Thank heaven we did not mention her name to him, and he evidently does not suspect. Pull yourself together and stumble through your part the best you can, dear, without attracting his attention. And then you know that he and you agree perfectly about the—cat," she added wickedly, and then she smiled quietly as she took her seat next to the blissful lover and the relentless judge of the school friend of her youth.

THE LADY OF THE CLUB.

"Poor naked wretches, wheresoe'er you are,
That bide the pelting of this pitiless storm,
How shall your houseless heads, and unfed sides,
Your loop'd, and window'd raggedness, defend you
From seasons such as these? O, I have ta'en
Too little care of this! Take physic, pomp;
Expose thyself to feel what wretches feel;
That thou may'st shake the super flux to them,
Show the heavens more just."

Shakespeare.

I.

The old and somewhat cynical saying, that philosophers and reformers can bear the griefs and woes of other people with a heroism and resignation worthy of their creeds, would have fitted the case of Roland Barker only when shorn of the intentional sting of sarcasm. It is, nevertheless, true that even his nobly-gifted nature, his tender heart, and his alert brain sometimes failed to grasp the very pith and point of his own arguments.

He was a wealthy man whose sympathies were earnestly with the poor and unfortunate. He believed that he understood their sufferings, their ambitions, and their needs; and his voice and pen were no more truly on the side of charity and brotherly kindness than was his purse.

It was no unusual thing for him to attend a meeting, address a club, or take part in a memorial service, where his was the only hand unused to toil, and where he alone bore all expense, and then—after dressing himself in the most approved and faultless manner—become the guest of honor at some fashionable entertainment. Indeed, he was a leader in fashion as well as in philosophy, and at once a hero in Avenue A and on Murray Hill.

On the evening of which I am about to tell you he had addressed a club of workingmen in their little dingy hall, taking as his subject "Realities of Life." He had sought to show them that poverty and toil are not, after all, the worst that can befall a man, and that the most acute misery dwells in palaces and is robed in purple.

He spoke with the feeling of one who had himself suffered—as, indeed, he had—from the unsympathetic associations of an uncongenial marriage. He portrayed, with deep feeling, the chill atmosphere of a loveless home, whose wealth and glitter and lustre could never thrill and enrapture the heart as might the loving hand-clasp in the bare, chill rooms where sympathy and affection were the companions of poverty.

I had admired his enthusiasm as he pictured the joy of sacrifice for the sake of those we love, and I had been deeply touched by his pathos—a pathos which I knew, alas, too well, sprang from a hungry heart—whether, as now, it beat beneath a simple coat of tweed or, as when hours later, it would still be the prisoner of its mighty longing, though clothed with elegance and seated at a banquet fit for princes.

The last words fell slowly from his lips, and his eyes were dimmed, as were the eyes of all about me. His voice, so full of feeling, had hardly ceased to throb when, far back in the little hall, arose a woman, thin and worn, and plainly clad, but showing traces of a beauty and refinement which had held their own and fought their way inch by inch in spite of poverty, anxiety, and tears. The chairman recognized her and asked her to the platform.

"No," she said, in a low, tremulous tone which showed at once her feeling and her culture—"no, I do not wish to take the platform; but since you ask for criticism of the kind speech we have just listened to, it has seemed to me that I might offer one, although I am a stranger to you all."

Her voice trembled, and she held firmly to the back of a chair in front of her. The chairman signified his willingness to extend to her the privilege of the floor, and there was slight applause. She bowed and began again slowly:

"I sometimes think that it is useless to ever try to make the suffering rich and the suffering poor understand each other. I do not question that the gentleman has tasted sorrow. All good men have. I do not question that his heart is warm and true and honest, and that he truly thinks what he has said; but"—and here her voice broke a little and her lip trembled—"but he does not know what real suffering is. He cannot. No rich man can." There was a movement of impatience in the room, and some one said, loud enough to be heard, "If she thinks money can bring happiness she is badly left."

There was a slight ripple of laughter at this, and even the serious face of Roland Barker grew almost merry for a moment. Then the woman went on, without appearing to have noticed the interruption:

"I do not want to seem ungracious, and heaven knows, no one could mean more kindly what I say; but he has said that money is not needed to make us happy—only love; and again he quotes that baseless old maxim, 'The love of money is the root of all evil.'" She paused, then went slowly on as if feeling her way and fearing to lose her hold upon herself: "I know it is a sad and cruel world even to the more fortunate, if they have hearts to feel and brains to think. To the unloving or unloved there must be little worth; but they at least are spared the agony that sits where love and poverty have shaken hands with death"—her voice broke, and there was a painful silence in the room— "where those who love are wrung and torn by all the thousand fears and apprehensions of ills that are to come to wife and child and friend. The day has passed when all this talk of poverty and love—that love makes want an easy thing to bear—the day has passed, I say, when sane men ought to think, or wise men speak, such cruel, false, and harmful words. He truly says that money without love cannot bring happiness; but that is only half the truth, for love with poverty can bring, does bring, the keenest agony that mortals ever bore."

There was a movement of dissent in the hall. She lifted her face a moment, contracted her lips, drew a long breath, and said:

"I will explain. Without the love, poverty were light enough to bear. What does it matter for one's self? It is the love that gives the awful sting to want, and makes its cruel fingers grip the throat as never vise or grappling-hook took hold, and torture with a keener zest than fiends their victims! Love and Poverty! *It is the combination that devils invented to make a hell on earth.*"

All eyes were fastened on her white face now, and she was rushing on, her words, hot and impassioned, striking firm on every point she made.

"Let me give you a case. In a home where comfort is—or wealth—a mother sits, watching by night and day the awful hand of Death reach nearer, closer to her precious babe, and nothing that skill or science can suggest will stay the hand or heal the aching heart; and yet there is comfort in the thought that all was done that love and wealth and skill could do, and that it was Nature's way. But take from her the comfort of that thought. She watches with the same poor, breaking heart, but with the knowledge, now, to keep her company, that science might, ah! *could*, push back the end, could even cure her babe if but the means to pay for skill and change and wholesome food and air were hers. Is that no added pang? Is poverty no curse to her?—a curse the deeper for her depth of love? The rich know naught of this. It gives to life its wildest agony, to love its deepest hurt."

She paused. There was a slight stir as if some one had thought to offer applause, and then the silence fell again, and she began anew, with shining eyes and cheeks aflame. She swayed a little as she spoke and clutched the chair as for support. Her voice grew hoarse, and trembled, and she fixed her gaze upon a vacant chair:

"But let me tell you of another case. A stone's throw from this hall, where pretty things are said week after week—and kindly meant, I know—of poverty and love—of the blessedness of these—there is a living illustration, worth more than all the theories ever spun, to tell you what 'realities of life' must be where love is great and poverty holds sway. Picture, with me, the torture and despair of a refined and cultured woman who watches hour by hour the long months through, and sees the creeping feet of mental wreck, and physical decay, and knows the mortal need of care and calm for him who is the whole of life to her, and for the want of that which others waste and hold as dross he must work on and on, hastening each day the end *he* does not see, which shall deprive him of all of life except the power for ill.... She will be worse than widowed and alone, for ever by her side sits Want, for him, tearing at every chord of heart and soul—not for herself—but for that dearer one, wrecked in the prime of life and left a clod endowed only with strength for cruel wrong, whose hand would sheath a knife in her dear heart and laugh with maniac glee at his mad deeds. She saw the end. She knew long months ago what was to be, if he must toil and strain his nerve and brain for need of that which goes from knave to knave, and hoards itself within cathedral walls, where wise men meet to teach the poor contentment with their lot! She knew *he* must not know; the knowledge of the shadow must be kept from *his* dear brain until the very end, by smiles, and cheer, and merry jest from her. Who dare tell *her* that riches are a curse? and prate of 'dross' and call on heaven to witness that its loss is only gain of joy and harbinger of higher, holier things? Who dare call *her* as witness for the bliss of poverty with love?"

She slowly raised her hand and, with a quick-drawn breath, pressed it against her side, and with her eyes still fastened on the vacant chair, and tears upon her cheeks, falling unchecked upon her heaving bosom, she held each listener silent and intent on every word she spoke. The time allotted anyone was long since overrun; but no one thought of that, and she went on:

"'With love!' Ah, there is where the iron can burn and scar and open every wound afresh each day, make poverty a curse, a blight, a scourge, a vulture, iron-beaked, with claws of burning steel, that leave no nerve untouched, no drop of blood unshed.

"'With love!' 'Tis there the hand of Poverty can deal the deadliest blows, and show, as nowhere else on earth, the value of that slandered, hoarded thing called wealth."

There blazed into her face a fierce, indignant light, her voice swelled out and struck upon the ear like fire-bells in the dead of night:

"'The root of evil!'—'poverty with love!' Hypocrisy, in purple velvet robed, behind stained glass, with strains of music falling on its ears, with table spread in banquet-hall below, bethought itself to argue thus to those itself had robbed; while, thoughtless of its meaning and its birth, the echo of its lying, treacherous words comes from the pallid lips of many a wretch whose life has been a failure and an agony because of that which he himself extols. A lie once born contains a thousand lives, and holds at bay the struggling, feeble truth, if but that lie be fathered by a priest and mothered by a throne—*as this one was!* 'The root of evil' is the spring of joy. Decry it those who will. And those who do *not* love, perchance, may laugh at all its need can mean; but to the loving, suffering poor bring no more cant, and cease to voice the hollow words of Ignorance and Hypocrisy. It is too cruel, and its deadly breath has long enough polluted sympathy and frozen up the springs of healthy thought, while sheathing venomed fangs in breaking hearts. Recast your heartless creeds! Your theories for the poor are built on these."

She sank back into her chair white and exhausted.

There was a wild burst of applause. A part of the audience, with that ear for sound and that lack of sense to be found in all such gatherings, had forgotten that it was not listening to a burst of eloquence which had been duly written out and committed to memory for the occasion.

But Roland Barker sprang to his feet, held both his hands up, to command silence, and said, in a scarcely audible voice, as he trembled from head to foot: "Hush, hush! She has told the truth! She has told the awful truth! I never saw it all before. Heaven help you to bear it. It seems to me I cannot!"

Several were pale and weeping. I turned to speak to the woman who had changed an evening's entertainment into a tragic scene; but she had slipped out during the excitement. I took Barker's arm and we walked towards the Avenue together. Neither of us spoke until we reached Madison Square. Here the poor fellow sank into a seat and pulled me down beside him.

"Don't talk to me about theories after that," he said. "Great God! I am more dead than alive. I feel fifty years older than when I went to that little hall to teach those people how to live by my fine philosophy, and I truly thought that I had tasted sorrow and found the key to resignation. Ye gods!"

"Perhaps you have," I said.

"Yes, yes," he replied, impatiently; "but suppose I had to face life day by day, hour by hour, as that woman pictured it—and she was a lady with as keen a sense of pain as I—what do you suppose my philosophy would do for me then? Do you think I could endure it? And I went there to teach those people how to suffer and be strong!"

"Look here, Barker," I said, "you'd better go home now and go to bed. You are cold and tired, and this won't help matters any."

"What will?" he asked.

I made no reply. When we reached his door he asked again:

"What will?"

I shook my head and left him standing in the brilliant hall of his beautiful home, dazed and puzzled and alone.

II.

The next time I met Roland Barker he grasped my hand and said excitedly: "I have found that woman! What she said is all true. My God! what is to be done? I feel like a strong man tied hand and foot, while devilish vultures feed on the flesh of living babes before my eyes!"

"Stop, Barker," I said; "stop, and go away for a while, or you will go mad. What have you been doing? Look at your hands; they tremble like the hands of a palsied man; and your face; why, Barker, your face is haggard and set, and your hair is actually turning gray! What in the name of all that's holy have you been doing?"

"Nothing, absolutely nothing!" he exclaimed "That is the trouble! What *can* I do? I tell you something is wrong, Gordon, something is desperately wrong in this world. Look at that pile of stone over there: millions of dollars are built into that. It is opened once each week, aired, cleaned, and put in order for a fashionable audience dressed in silk and broadcloth. They call it a church, but it is simply a popular club house, which, unlike other club houses, hasn't the grace to pay its own taxes. They use that club house, let us say, three hours in all, each week, for what? To listen to elaborate music and fine-spun theories about another world. They are asked to, and they give money to send these same theories to nations far away, who—to put it mildly—are quite as well off without them. Then that house is closed for a week, and those who sat there really believe that they have done what is right by their fellow-men! Their natural consciences, their sense of right and justice, have been given an anaesthetic. 'The poor ye have with you always,' they are taught to believe, is not only true, but *right*. I tell you, Gordon, it is all perfectly damnable, and it seems to me that I cannot bear it when I remember that woman."

"She is only one of a great many," I suggested.

Roland Barker groaned: "My God! that is the trouble—so many that the thing seems hopeless. And to think that on every one of even these poor souls is laid another burden that that stone spire may go untaxed!"

"Barker," I said, laying my hand on his arm, "tell me what has forced all this upon you with such a terrible weight just now."

"Not here, not now," he said. "I have written it down just as she told it to me—you know I learned stenography when I began taking an interest in public meetings. Well, I've just been copying those notes out. They are in my pocket," he said, laying his hand on his breast. "They seem to burn my very soul. I would not dare to trust myself to read them to you here. Come home with me."

When we were seated in his magnificent library, he glanced about him, and with a wave of his hand said, with infinite satire: "You will notice the striking appropriateness of the surroundings and the subject."

"No doubt," I said. "I have often noticed that before, especially the last time I heard a sermon preached to three of the Vanderbilts, two Astors, five other millionaires, and about sixty more consistent Christians, all of whom were wealthy. The subject was Christ's advice to the rich young man, 'Sell all thou hast and give to the poor.' But never mind; go on; the day has passed when deed and creed are supposed to hold the slightest relation to each other; and what is a $20,000 salary for if not to buy sufficient ability to explain it all sweetly away and administer, at the same time, an anæsthetic to the natural consciences of men?"

I settled myself in a large Turkish chair on one side of the splendidly carved table; he stood on the other side sorting a manuscript. Presently he began reading it. "'When I married Frank Melville he was strong and grand and brave; a truer man never lived. He had been educated for the law. His practice was small, but we were able to live very well on what he made, and the prospect for the future was bright. We loved each other—but, ah! there are no words to tell that. We worshipped each other as only two who have been happily mated can ever understand. We lived up to his salary. Perhaps you will say that that was not wise. We thought it was. A good appearance, a fairly good appearance at least, was all that we could make, and to hold his own in his profession, this was necessary. You know how that is. A shabby-looking man soon loses his hold on paying clients. Of course he would not dress well and allow me to be ill-clad. He—he loved me. We were never able to lay by anything; but we were young and strong and hopeful—and we loved each other.'" Barker's voice trembled. He looked at me a moment and then said very low: "If you could have seen her poor, tired, beautiful eyes when she said that."

"I can imagine how she looked," I said. "She had a face one remembers."

After a little he went on: "We had both been brought up to live well. Our friends were people of culture, and we—it will sound strange to you for me to say that our love and devotion were the admiration and talk of all of them.

"'By-and-by I was taken ill. My husband could not bear to think of me as at home alone, suffering He stayed with me a great deal. I did not know that he was neglecting his business; I think he did not realize it then; he thought he could make it all up; he was strong and—he loved me. At last the doctors told him that I should die if he did not take me away; I ought to have an ocean voyage. It almost killed him that he could not give me that. We had not the money. He took me away a little while where I could breathe the salt air, and the good it did me made his heart only the sadder when he saw that it was true that all I needed was an ocean voyage. The climate of his home was slowly killing me. We bore it as long as we dared, and I got so weak that he almost went mad. Then we moved here, where my health was good. But it was a terrible task to get business; there were so many others like him, all fighting, as if for life, for money enough to live on from day to day. The strain was too much for him, and just as he began to gain a footing he fell ill, and—and if we had had money enough for him to take a rest then, and have proper care, good doctors, and be relieved from immediate anxiety, he would have gotten well, with my care—I loved him so! But as it was—' Shall I show you the end?" Barker stopped, he was trembling violently, his eyes were full of tears. I waited. Presently he said, huskily: "Shall I tell you, Gordon, what I saw? I have not gotten over it yet. She laid her finger on her lips and motioned me to follow. The room where we had been was poor and bare. She took a key from her bosom, opened a door, and went in. I followed. Sitting in the only comfortable chair—which had been handsome once—was a magnificent-looking man, so far as mere physical proportions can make one that.

"'Darling,' she said tenderly, as if talking to a little child. 'Darling, I have brought you a present. Are you glad?'

"She handed him a withered rose that I had carelessly dropped as I went in.

"He arose, bowed to me when she presented me, waved me to his chair, took the flower, looked at her with infinite love, and said: 'To-morrow, little wife; wait till to-morrow.'

"Then he sat down, evidently unconscious of my presence, and gazed steadily at her for a moment, seeming to forget all else and to struggle with some thought that constantly eluded him. She patted his hand as if he were a child, smiling through her heart-break all the while, kissed him, and motioned me to precede her from the room.

"When she came out she locked the door carefully behind her, sank into a chair, covered her face with her hands, and sobbed as if her heart would break. After a while she said: 'A little money would have saved, him and now it is too late, too late. Sometimes he is violent, sometimes like that. The doctors say the end is not far off, and that any moment he may kill me, and afterwards awake to know it! It is all the result of poverty *with love!* she said. Then, passionately: 'If I did not love him so I could bear it, but *I cannot, I cannot!* And how will *he* bear it if he ever harms me—and I not there to help him?'"

Barker stepped to the window to hide his emotion. Presently he said, in a voice that trembled: "If she did not love him so she could let him go to some—asylum; but she knows the end is sure, and not far off, and that the gleams of light he has are when he sees her face. She has parted with everything that made life attractive to keep food and warmth for him. She is simply existing now from day to day—one constant agony of soul and sense—waiting for the end. She allowed me to take a doctor to see him; I would have come for you, but you were out of town. He only confirmed what others had told her a year ago. He advised her to have him put in a safe place before he did some violence; but she refused, and made us promise not to interfere. She said he would be able to harm no one but her, if he became violent at the last, and she was ready for that. It was easier far to live that way and wait for that each day than to have him taken away where he would be unhappy and perhaps ill-treated. He needed her care and love beside him every hour, and she —she needed nothing."

Here Barker flung himself into a chair and let his head fall on his folded arms on the table.

"That is the way love makes poverty easy to bear," he said, bitterly, after a time, and his trembling hands clinched tight together.

"Did you give her any money?" I asked.

He groaned. "Yes, yes, I—that is, I left some on the table under her sewing. She isn't the kind of woman one can offer charity. She—"

"No," I said, "she isn't, and beside, for the pain that tortures her it is too late now for money to help. Only it may relieve her somewhat to feel sure that she can get what he needs to eat and wear and to keep him warm and allow her to be free from the necessity of outside work. I am glad you left the money. But—but—Barker, do you think she will use it, coming that way and from a stranger?"

He looked up forlornly. "No, I don't," he said; "and yet she may. I will hope so; but if she does, what then? The terrible question will still remain just where it was. That is no way to solve it; we can't bail out the ocean with a thimble. And what an infamous imposition all this talk is of 'resignation' to such as she; for her terrible calm, as she talked to me, had no hint of resignation in it. She is simply, calmly, quietly desperate now—and she is one of many." He groaned aloud.

"Will you take me there the next time you go?" I asked.

"She said I must not come back; she could not be an object of curiosity— nor allow him to be. She said that she allowed me to come this time because on the night we first saw her she had stepped into that little hall to keep herself from freezing in her thin clothes as she was making her way home, and she saw that I was earnest in what I said, and she stayed to listen—" his voice broke again.

Just then the drapery was drawn back, and his wife, superbly robed, swept in, bringing a bevy of girls.

"Oh, Mr. Barker," said one, gayly, "you don't know what you missed to-night by deserting our theatre party; it was all so real—love in rags, you know, and all that sort of thing; only I really don't like to see *quite* so much attention paid to the 'Suffering poor,' with a big S, and the lower classes generally. I think the stage can do far better than that, don't you? But it is the new fad, I suppose, and after all I fancy it doesn't do much harm, only as it makes that sort of people more insufferably obtrusive about putting their ill-clad, bad-smelling woes before the rest of us. What a beautiful vase this is, Mrs. Barker! May I take it to the light?"

"Certainly, my dear," laughed Mrs. Barker; "and I agree with you, as usual. I think it is an exquisite vase—and that the stage is becoming demoralized. It is pandering to the low taste for representations of low life. I confess I don't like it. That sort of people do not have the feelings to be hurt—the fine sensibilities and emotions attributed to them. Those grow up in refined and delicate surroundings. That is what I often tell Roland when he insists upon making himself unhappy over some new 'case' of destitution. I tell him to send them five dollars by mail and not to worry himself, and I won't allow him to worry me with his Christie-street emotions."

Barker winced, and I excused myself and withdrew, speculating on certain phases of delicacy of feeling and fine sensibility.

III.

I did not see Barker again for nearly three weeks, when one night my bell was rung with unusual violence, and I heard an excited voice in my hall. "Be quick, John; hurry," it said, "and tell the doctor I must see him at once. Tell him it is Roland Barker."

John had evidently demurred at calling me at so late an hour.

"All right, Barker; I'll be down in a moment," I called from above. "No, come up. You can tell me what is the matter while I dress. Is it for yourself? There, go in that side room, I can hear you, and I'll be dressed in a moment."

"Hurry, hurry," he said, excitedly, "I'll tell you on the way. I have my carriage. Don't wait to order yours, only hurry, hurry, hurry."

Once in the carriage, I said: "Barker, you are going to use yourself up, this way. You can't keep this sort of thing up much longer. You'd better go abroad."

"Drive faster," he called, to the man on top. Then to me, "If you are not the first doctor there? there will be a dreadful scene. They will most likely arrest her for murder."

"Whom?" said I. "You have told me nothing, and how can I prevent that if a murder has been committed?"

"By giving her a regular death certificate," said he, coolly, "saying that you attended the case, and that it was a natural death. I depend upon you, Gordon; it would be simply infamous to make her suffer any more. I cannot help her now, but you can, you *must*. No one will know the truth but us, and afterwards we can help her—to forget. She is not an old woman; there may be something in life for her yet."

"Is it the Lady of the Club?" I asked. We had always called her that "What has she done?"

"Yes," he said, "it is the 'Lady of the Club.' and she has poisoned her husband."

"Good God!" exclaimed I; "and you want me to give her a regular death certificate and say I attended the case?"

"You must," he said; "it would be infamous not to. She could not bear it any longer. She found herself breaking down, and she would not leave him alive without her care and love. He had become almost helpless, except when short violent spells came on. These left him exhausted. He almost killed her in the last one. Her terror was that he would do so and then regain his reason—that he would know it afterwards and perhaps be dragged through the courts. She had been working in a chemist's office, it seems, when she was able to do anything. She took some aconitine, and to-night she put everything in perfect order, gave him the best supper she could, got him to bed, and then—gave him that. She sent for me and told me as calmly as— God! it was the calm of absolute desperation. She sat there when I went in, holding his poor dead hand and kissing it reverently. She laid it down and told me what I tell you. There was not a tear, a moan, a sigh. She said: 'Here is the money you left—all except what I paid for his supper to-night. We had gotten down to that before I had the chance to steal the poison or the courage to give it to him. I had not meant to use any of the money; the rest is here. I would like it used—if you are willing—to bury him decently, not in the Potter's Field, and I would like—if you will take the trouble—to have it done absolutely privately. We have borne enough. I cannot bear for even his ashes to be subjected to any further humiliation.'"

Roland Barker paused to command himself. "Of course I promised her," he went on, after a time. "She does not realize that she may be arrested and have his poor body desecrated to find the cause of death. That would make her insane—even if— Drive faster!" he called out again to the man outside. When we reached the house he said: "Be prepared to see her perfectly calm. It is frightful to witness, and I tremble for the result later on."

When we knocked on her door there was no response. I pushed it open and entered first. The room was empty. We went to the inner doer and rapped gently, then louder. There was no sound. Barker opened the door, and then stepped quickly back and closed it. "She is kneeling there by his bed," he said; "write the certificate here and give it to me. Then I will bring an undertaker and—he and I can attend to everything else. I did want you to see her. I think you should give her something to make her sleep. That forced calm will make her lose her mind. She is so shattered you would not recognize her."

"Stay here, Barker," I said; "I want to see her alone for a moment. I will tell her who I am and that you brought me—if I need to."

He eyed me sharply, but I stepped hastily into the inner room. I touched the shoulder and then the forehead of the kneeling form. It did not move. "Just as I expected," I muttered, and lifting the lifeless body in my arms I laid it gently beside her husband. In one hand she held the vial from which she had taken the last drop of the deadly drug, and clasped in the other her husband's fingers. She had been dead but a few moments, and both she and her husband were robed for the grave.

When I returned to the outer room I found Barker with a note in his hand, and a shocked and horrified look on his face. He glanced up at me through his tears.

"We were too late," he said. "She left this note for me. I found it here on the table. She meant to do it all along, and that is why she was so calm and had no fears for herself."

"I thought so when you told me what she had done," said I.

"Did you? I did not for a moment, or I would have stayed and tried to reason her out of it."

"It is best as it is," said I, "and you could not have reasoned her out of it. It was inevitable—after the rest. Take this certificate too; you will need both."

When all was safely over, as we drove home from the new graves two days later, Barker said: "Is this the solution?"

I did not reply.

Presently he said: "To the dead, who cannot suffer, we can be kind and shield them even from themselves. Is there no way to help the living? A few hundred dollars, two short years ago, would have saved all this, and there was no way for her to get it. She knew it *all* then, and there was no help!"

"Why did she not, in such a case as that, push back her pride and go to some one? There must be thousands who would have gladly responded to such a call as that," I argued.

He buried his face in his hands for a moment and shuddered. At last he said: "She did—she went to three good men, men who had known, been friendly with, admired her and her husband. Two of them are worth their millions, the other one is rich. She only asked to borrow, and promised to repay it herself if she had to live and work after he were dead to do it!"

He paused.

"You do not mean to tell me that they refused—and they old friends and rich?" I asked, amazed.

"I mean to say just this: they one and all made some excuse; they did not let her have it."

"She told them what the doctors said, and of her fears?"

"She did," he answered, sadly.

"And yet you say they are good men!" I exclaimed, indignantly.

"Good, benevolent, charitable, every one of them," he answered.

"Were you one of them, Barker?" I asked, after a moment's pause.

"Thank God, no!" he replied. "But perhaps in some other case I have done the same, if I only knew the whole story. Those men do not know this last, you must remember."

"And the worst of it is, we dare not tell them," said I, as we parted.

"No, we dare not," he replied, and left me standing with the copy of the burial certificate in my hand.

"Natural causes?" I said to myself, looking at it. "Died of natural causes—the brutality and selfishness of man—and poverty with love. *Natural* causes! Yes." And I closed my office door and turned out the light.

UNDER PROTEST.

"This is my story, sir; a trifle, indeed, I assure you.

"Much more, perchance, might be said; but I hold him, of all men, most lightly Who swerves from the truth in his tale."

Bret Harte.

When the new family moved into, and we were told had bought, the cottage nearest our own, we were naturally interested in finding out what kind of people they were, and whether we had gained or lost by the change of neighbors.

In a summer place like this it makes a good deal of difference just what kind of people live so near to you that when you are sitting on your veranda and they are swinging in hammocks on theirs, the most of the conversation is common property, unless you whisper, and one does not want to spend three or four months of each year mentally and verbally tiptoeing about one's own premises. Then, on the other hand, there are few less agreeable situations to be placed in than to be forced to listen to confidences or quarrels with which you have nothing whatever to do, or else be deprived of the comforts and pleasures of out-door life, to secure which you endure so many other annoyances.

Our new neighbors were, therefore, as you will admit, of the utmost interest and importance to us, and I was naturally very much pleased, at the end of the first week, when I returned one day from a fishing party, from which my wife's headache had detained her, by the report she gave me of their attitude toward each other. (From her glowing estimate, I drew rose-colored pictures of their probable kindliness and generosity toward others.) Up to this time they had been but seldom outside of their house, and we had not gathered much information of their doings, except the fact that a good deal of nice furniture had come, and they appeared to be greatly taken up in beautifying and arranging their cottage. This much promised well, so far as it went; but we had not lived to our time of life not to find out, long ago, that the most exquisitely appointed houses sometimes lack the one essential feature; that is, ladies and gentlemen to occupy them.

"They are lovely!" said my wife, the moment I entered the door, before I had been able to deposit my fishing-tackle and ask after her headache. "They are lovely; at least he is," she amended. "I am sure we shall be pleased with them; or, at least, with him. A man as careful of, and attentive to, his wife as he is can't help being an agreeable neighbor."

"Good!" said I. "How did you find out? And how is your headache?—Had a disgusting time fishing. Glad you did not go. Sun was hot; breeze was hot; boatman's temper was a hundred and twenty in the shade; bait wouldn't stay on the hooks, and there weren't any fish any way. But how did you say your head is?"

"My head?" said my wife, with that retrospective tone women have, which seemed to indicate that if she had ever had a head, and if her head had ever ached, and if headache was a matter of sufficient importance to remember, in all human probability it had recovered in due time. "My head? Oh, yes— Oh, it is all right; but you really never did see any one so tractable as that man. And adaptable! Why, it is a perfect wonder. Of course I had no business to look or listen; but I did. I just couldn't help it. The fact is, I thought they were quarrelling at first, and I almost fainted. I said to myself, 'If they are that kind of people we will sell out. I will not live under the constant drippings of ill-temper.' Quarrelling ought to be a penitentiary offence; that is, I mean the bickerings and naggings most people dignify by that name. I could endure a good, square, stand-up and knock down quarrel, that had some character to it; but the eternal differences, often expressed by the tones of voice only, I can't stand." I smiled an emphatic assent, and my wife went on.

"Well, I must confess his tones of voice are, at times, against him; but I'm not sure that it is not due to the distance. *All* of his tones may not carry this far. I'm sure they don't, for when I first heard him, and made up my mind that it was a horrid, common, plebeian little row, I went to the west bedroom window—you know it looks directly into their kitchen—and what do you suppose I saw?"

The question was so sudden and wholly unexpected, and my mental apparatus was so taken up with the story that I found myself with no ideas whatever on the subject Indeed I do not believe that my wife wanted me to guess what she saw, half so much as she wanted breath; but I gave the only reply which the circumstances appeared to admit of, and which, I was pleased to see, in spite of its seeming inadequacy, was as perfectly satisfactory to the blessed little woman as if it had been made to order and proven a perfect fit.

"I can't imagine," said I.

"Of course you can't," she replied, pushing my crossed legs into position, and seating herself on my knees.

"Of course you can't. A man couldn't. Well, it seems their servant left last night, and that blessed man was washing the dishes this morning. The difference of opinion had been over which one of them should do it."

"Why, the confounded brute!" said I. "He is a good deal better able to do it than she is. She looks sick, and so long as he has no business to attend to down here, he has as much time as she and a good deal more strength to do that kind of work."

"Well, I just knew you'd look at it that way," said my wife, with an inflection of pride and admiration which indicated that I had made a ten strike of some kind, of which few men—and not many women—would be capable.

"But that was not it at all," continued she.

I began laboriously to readjust my mental moorings to this seemingly complicated situation, and was on the verge of wondering why my wife was so pleased with me for simply making a mistake, when she began again, after giving me a little pat of unqualified satisfaction and sympathy.

"They both wanted to do it. She said she wasn't a bit tired and could do it alone just as well as not, and he'd break the glasses with his funny, great, big fingers; and he said he'd be careful not to break anything, and that the dish-water would spoil her hands."

"Good," said I, "I shall like the fellow. I———"

"Of course you will," my wife broke in, enthusiastically; "but that isn't all. I went to sleep after that, and later on was awakened by a loud—and as I thought at the time—a very angry voice. I went to the window again only to see a laughing scuffle between them over the potato-knife. She wanted to scrape them and he wanted to scrape them. Of course he got the knife, and it really did look too comical to see him work with those little bulbs. He put his whole mind on them, and he didn't catch her picking over the berries until she was nearly done. Then he scolded again. He said he did the potatoes to keep her from getting her thumb and forefinger black, and here she was with her whole hand covered with berry stain. He seemed really vexed, and I must say his voice doesn't carry this far as if he was half as nice as he is. I think there ought to be a chair of voices attached to every school-house—so to speak—and the result of the training made one of the tests of admission to the colleges of the country. Don't you?"

Again I was wholly unprepared for her sudden question, and was only slowly clambering around the idea she had suggested, so I said—somewhat irrelevantly, no doubt—"It may be."

She looked at me for a moment without speaking, and then said, as she got up and crossed the room: "You didn't hear a word I said, and you don't begin to appreciate that man anyway."

"I did hear you, dear," I protested; "I was listening as hard as I could—and awfully interested—but a fellow can't skip along at that rate and have well-matured views on tap without a moment's warning. You've got to be like the noble ladies in the 'Lay of the Last Minstrel,' 'and give me heart and give me time.' Now *they* understood men. We're slow."

She laughed and tied the last pink bow in the lace of a coquettish little white gown and dragged me out on the veranda.

Our new neighbors were out ahead of us.

"I don't think so at all, Margaret," we heard him say, as we took our chairs near the edge of the porch to catch any stray breeze that might be wandering our way.

"Sh—," we heard her say; "don't talk so loud. They will think you are going to scalp me."

"Oh, don't bother about the neighbors; let 'em hear," said he, "let 'em think. Who cares? If they haven't got anything better to do than sit around and think, they'd better move away from our neighborhood."

"Sh—said she again, looking at him with a good deal of emphasis in her eyes.

"Well, it is too bad, isn't it?" acquiesced he, in a much lower voice, and one from which every vestige of the tone of protest had vanished.

"It *is* too bad that these summer cottages are built so close together that you can't tie your shoes without being overheard by the folks next door? It makes me nervous. I feel as if I had to sit up straight all the time and smile like a crocodile, or else run the risk of being misunderstood."

"It *is* trying, dear," she said, "and destroys a good deal of the comfort and ease of one's outing."

"Nothing of the kind," began he, so explosively as to make my wife jump.

"Sh—," whispered the lady next door, but he went on.

"Nothing of the kind. I don't let it bother me in the least. They can attend to their own affairs, and I——"

"Sh—," said his wife; "suppose we walk down to the beach." She began to adjust her wrap.

"It is a good deal more comfortable here," he protested, "and besides I'm tired."

"So you are, of course," she said, regretfully. "I forgot. Such unusual work for a man would tire him;" and she loosened the lace veil she had drawn over her head and reseated herself.

"Well, are you ready?" questioned he, clapping on his hat and suddenly starting down the steps.

"Ready for what?" asked she, in surprise.

"The deuce, Margaret. I thought you said that you were going to the beach!"

She got up, readjusted her veil, took her wrap on her arm, and ran lightly after him.

"I wonder if I shall need this wrap?" she said as she passed our gate.

"Heavens! no," he replied, "and it will heat you all up to carry it. Here, give it to me. I don't see what on earth you brought it for. I'm certainly hot enough without loading me up with this."

"I will carry it," she said, cheerfully; "I don't feel the heat on my arm as you do—or I'll run back and leave it on the porch. You walk slowly. I can easily catch up."

She started; but he took the shawl from her, threw it lightly over his shoulder, and, pulling her hand through his arm, said gayly, and in the most compliant tone: "It isn't very warm. I won't notice this little thing and, besides, you'll need it down there, as like as not."

When they were out of hearing my wife drew a long breath and said: "I wonder if we ever sound like that to other people?—and yet, they seem to be devoted to each other," she added hastily.

"They are, no doubt," said I, "only he appears to be a chronic kicker."

"A comic what?" said my wife, in so loud a tone that I involuntarily exclaimed "Sh—!"

We both laughed. Then she said: "But really, dear, I didn't understand what you said he was. There doesn't seem to me to be anything comic about him, though. And——"

"Comic! Well, I should think not," said I. "I should think it would be anything but comic to that little woman to go through that sort of thing every time she opened her mouth. What I said was that he seems to be a chronic kicker, and I might add—with some show of fairness—that he impresses me as the champion of Kicktown at that."

"Sh—," laughed my wife, "they're coming back."

"I don't agree with you at all. There is no need to do anything of the kind," were the first words we heard from a somewhat distant couple, and my wife concluded that our new neighbors were not very far off. "It would be no end of trouble for you. You'd get all tired out; and besides, what do we owe to the Joneses that makes it necessary for you to disturb all our little comforts to ask them down here?" he continued. We could not hear her reply; but his protest and evident deep dissatisfaction with the whole scheme went bravely on.

She passed into the house and left him on the steps. When she came out a few moments later he said, sweetly: "As I was just saying, it will be quite a diversion for you to see the girls, and I'd enjoy the old man hugely. He's a jolly old coon; and then we owe it to them after all they did for you."

"What girls? What old man is a jolly coon?" asked she, in an utterly bewildered tone.

"Margaret! The Joneses, of course. Whom have we been talking about for the last half-hour?" exploded he.

"Oh," said she, having evidently quite given over asking the Joneses, and become occupied with other thoughts, "I thought the idea did not please you. But I'm so glad. It will do you good to have him here, and I shall be delighted."

"Do me good!" exploded he. "Do me good! Tiresome old bore, if there ever was one. Women are queer fish to deal with, but I'm sure I don't care whom you invite here."

Our neighbors withdrew for the night and we sighed with relief. About two o'clock my wife touched me to find if I was asleep. The movement was so stealthy that I inferred at once that there were burglars in the house. I was wide awake in an instant.

"What is it?" I whispered.

"Well, I'm glad you're awake. I want to know what that was you called the man next door. I forgot what it was, and I couldn't sleep for trying to remember."

I laughed. "I believe I said that he impressed me as one so addicted to the reprehensible habit of protest—on general principles, as it were—that it had now become the normal condition of his mental constitution."

"You didn't say any such thing," said she. "You—"

"I believe that at the time of which you speak I allowed myself to be guilty of a habit you do not wholly admire; but I really had no idea it would keep you awake. I used slang. I said that he was a chronic kicker, and—"

"That's it! That's it!" exclaimed she, with deep satisfaction. "He's a 'chronic kicker.' Well, if you'll believe me, he hasn't stopped kicking long enough to say his prayers decently since we went to bed. First about what time it was; then about which room they'd sleep in; then there was too much cover; then the windows were wrong; then—oh, heavens!—I wonder if he kicks in his sleep? He always comes around to reason in time; but if there was ever anything more maddening to meet than that constant wall of protest—for the sake of protest—I don't know what it could be."

"Nor—I," said I, half asleep.

Presently her hand grasped mine vigorously, and I sprang up startled, for I had been sound asleep again. "What's the matter?" I said, in a loud tone.

"Sh—," whispered my wife. "Don't speak in that tone. I'd rather people would think you stayed out nights, than to suppose you stayed at home and nagged me. He's at it again. I'd most gone to sleep and his voice nearly scared the life out of me. She wanted to close the window. He objected, of course; said he'd smother—sh—"

Just then we heard our neighbor's wife ask sleepily: "What are you doing, dear?"

"Closing this detestable window. Lets in too much salt air. 'Fraid you'll get chilled. I am. Where's another blanket?"

The window went down with a bang, and we heard no more of our neighbors that night. But the next morning the same thing began again, and I do not believe that during that entire summer he ever agreed with his wife the first time she spoke, nor failed to come around to her view after he took time to think it over. I remember when I was introduced to him, a week later, his wife said: "This is our nearest neighbor, you know, Thomas, and—"

"No, he isn't, Margaret; the people back of us are nearer," he said. Then to me: "Pleased to meet you. I believe our wives have become quite good friends. I'm very glad for Margaret's sake, too. It's dull for her with only an old fellow like me to entertain her, and she not very well. And then, as she says, you are our nearest neighbor, and we really ought not to be too ceremonious at such a place as this."

"I thought, Thomas," suggested his wife, "that you said one could not be too particular. Why, you quite blustered when I first told you I had made advances to some of the other—"

"Nonsense! I did nothing of the kind," broke in he. "What on earth ever put such an idea into your head, Margaret? You know I always say that without pleasant neighbors, and friendly relations with them, a summer cottage is no place for a white man to live."

My wife hastened to change the subject. Nothing on earth is more distasteful to her than a family contest, of even a very mild type, especially when the tones of voice seem to express more of indignation and a desire to override, than a mere difference of opinion. She thought the surf a safe subject.

"Was not the water lovely to-day? You were in, I suppose?" she inquired of our neighbor's wife.

"Yes, we were in," she began, enthusiastically. "It was perfect and—"

"I don't know what you call perfect," broke in he, "I called it beastly. It was so cold I felt like a frog when I got out, and you looked half frozen. The fact is, this is too far north to bathe for pleasure in the surf. It may be good for one's health, but it is anything but pleasant. Now at Old Point Comfort it is different. I like it there."

"Why, James," said his wife, "I thought you preferred this because of the more bracing and exhilarating effect."

After a little more objection, which he seemed to think firmly established his independence, he ended his remarks thus:

"Of course, as you say, it is more bracing. Yes, that's a fact, Margaret. I couldn't help noticing when I came out this morning that I felt like a new man, and you—why, 'pon my word, you looked as bright and rosy as a girl of sixteen. Oh, the surf here is great. It really is. I like it; don't you?"

This last he had addressed to me. I was so occupied in a study of, and so astonished by, the facility with which he took his mental flops, after enjoying his little "kick," that I was taken off my feet by his sudden appeal to me, and was quite at a loss for a reply which would do justice to the occasion, and at the same time put a stop to the contest between husband and wife.

But, as usual, my wife hastened to my rescue and covered my confusion by her gay little laugh and explanation.

"Ha, ha, ha," she laughed, "you have caught my husband napping already. I know exactly where he was. He was lumbering along through an elaborate speculation on, and a comparison of, the relative merits of—" here she began telling them off on her fingers to the great amusement of our neighbors— "first, fresh and salt water bathing; second, the method, time, place, and condition of each as affected by the moon, stars, and Gulf Stream. He was, most likely, climbing over Norway with a thermometer, or poking a test-tube of some kind into the semi-liquefaction which passes itself off as water to those unfortunates who are stranded along the shores of the Mississippi. Just wait; one of these days he will get down to our discussion and he'll agree with us when he gets there. But don't hurry him."

We all joined in the laugh at my expense; and I remarked that I had served so long as a target for my wife's fun that even if I could skip around, mentally, at as lively a rate as she seemed to expect, I would pretend that I couldn't, in order not to deprive her of her chief source of amusement. At this point our neighbor's new cook came to the edge of their porch and asked her mistress if she might speak to her for a moment. She arose to go.

"Oh, thunder, Margaret, I hope you don't intend to allow that worthless girl to call you home every time you go any place. Tell her to wait. It can't be much she wants," said our neighbor.

"Jane," said his wife sweetly, reseating herself, "you can wait until I come home. It won't be long."

"I wonder if you'd better do that, Margaret," said he, just as our wives had begun to discuss something relative to housekeeping. "Jane is a good girl, and she wouldn't call you if it were not something important, Don't you think we had better go at once?"

"I did think so," said she, and bidding us goodnight our neighbors crossed the lawn and re-entered their own door and closed it for the night.

After a long pause my wife said, in a stage whisper: "I suppose it is his way of showing that he is 'boss,' as the boys say—the final appeal in his own household—his idea of the dignity of the masculine prerogative."

A sudden stop. I thought she expected me to say something, so I began:

"I don't know. I doubt it. It looks to me like a case of—"

"Don't! don't!" exclaimed my wife, in tragic accents "oh, *don't* catch it. I really couldn't live with a chronic objector. Anything else. I really believe I could stand any other phase of bullying better than that—to feel that at any minute I am liable to run against a solid wall of 'I don't agree with you!' If it were *real* I wouldn't mind it so much; but to hear that man 'kick,' as you say, just for the sake of asserting himself, and then come around as he does, is perfectly maddening. The very first symptom I see in you I shall look upon it as a danger signal—I'll move."

At that moment, before our quiet little laugh, at their expense, had died away, there floated out from the bedroom window of our neighbors' cottage, this refrain:

"Well, goodness knows, Margaret, *I* didn't want to come home. I knew it was all perfect nonsense. If you—"

My wife suddenly arose, took me by the hand and said quite seriously: "Come in the house, dear. This atmosphere is too unwholesome to endure any longer."

The next day she said to me, "Let's go to Old Point Comfort next year."

"All right," said I; "but what shall we do with the cottage? You know we hold the lease for another year, with the 'refusal' to buy."

"Rent it to your worst enemy, or, better still, get him to buy it. Just think of the exquisite revenge you could take that way. Twenty-four hours every day, for four long months each year, to know that you had him planted next door to a 'chronic kicker.' Or don't you hate anybody bad enough for that?" and my wife actually shuddered.

"I don't believe I do, dear," said I; "but I'll do my level best to *rent* it to him for one season. You know I wouldn't care to murder him; if he's hopelessly maimed I'll be satisfied."

We both laughed; but the next day I advertised the lease of a cottage for sale very cheap, and gave as a reason my desire to go where there were fewer people. I think this will catch my enemy. He likes a crowd, and he'd enjoy nothing better than to feel that I was forced to pay half of his rent. So I marked the paper and sent it to him, and confidently await the result.

FOR THE PROSECUTION.

"So deeply inherent is it in this life of ours that men have to suffer for each other's sins, so inevitably diffusive is human sufferings that even Justice makes its victims, and we can conceive no retribution that does not spread beyond its mark in pulsations of unmerited pain."—George Eliot.

I.

Shortly after Fred Mathews began the practice of law he was elected to the office of Prosecuting Attorney in the Western town to which he had gone when first admitted to the bar.

Of course, every law student becomes familiar with the jests and gibes cast at the members of the profession as men who are peculiarly economical of the truth. He smiles with those who hint that a lawyer is always lavish of advice that leads to litigation.

That students of Blackstone and Coke hear much merrymaking over and some serious criticism of the quibbles to which the best of them are supposed to resort—of making little of real evidence and much of trivialities—goes without saying. Nor are they unaware of the fact—alas! sometimes too well founded upon strong evidence—that the general public appears to be convinced that laws are made for the purpose of shielding the rich and oppressing the poor or unfortunate.

No student of average ability enters practice uninformed that there is a widespread belief that a man of social position or financial power has little to fear as a result of his misdeeds, while his less fortunate neighbor could not hope to escape the worst legal consequences of his most trivial lapse from rectitude.

Fred Mathews had made up his mind—as many a young fellow had done before him—that he would do everything in his power to hold the scales of justice level.

He determined that such ability as he possessed should be used for the benefit of society, and that neither bribe nor threat should ever entice him from the strict performance of his duty to the profession which he had entered. He would never accept a case in which he did not honestly believe. No man's money should buy him and no man's wrath intimidate. In short, he intended to be a lawyer with a conscience as well as a man of integrity, no matter what the result might be.

He made so good a beginning in the first two years of his practice that it was at the end of the third, when he found himself holding the office of Prosecuting Attorney, with a record clean, and fair sailing ahead, that a piece of news which came to him caused him to doubt himself for the first time.

The shock of that doubt thrilled every fibre in his nature, for with it came the one fear that is terrible to a brave mind which is aroused for the first time to its own possibilities—the fear to trust itself—the dread lest it betray its own higher nature under the pressure of old habits of thought or new social problems.

Right and wrong had always seemed to him to have the most decided and clear-cut outlines. He had never thought of himself as standing before them unable to distinguish their boundaries. He had felt that he could answer bravely enough the question: "What would you do if required to choose between honor and dishonor?" It was a strange thing to him that his present perplexity should grow out of a simple burglary case. There did not appear to him, at first, to be more than one side to such a case. He was the Prosecuting Attorney. A store had been robbed. Among other things a sealskin sacque was taken. By means of this cloak the burglary had been traced—it was claimed—to a certain young man high in social life. The duties of his office had led the State's attorney to prosecute the investigation with his usual vigor and impartiality until he had succeeded beyond his fairest hopes. Indeed, the chain of evidence now in his possession was so strong and complete that he—for the first time in his career—recognized that he shrank from using the testimony at his command.

He felt that it was his duty to cause to be apprehended a young man who had up to the present time borne a spotless reputation; who had been a fellow student at college; whose social position was that of a leader, and who was soon to marry one of the most charming girls in the town. The situation was painful, but Fred Mathews felt that his own honor was at stake quite as truly as was that of his old schoolfellow. Here was his first opportunity to show that he held his duty above his desires. Here was the first case in which social influence and financial power were on the side of a criminal whom it was his duty to prosecute to the end.

His professional pride, as well as his honor, was enlisted; for this was the third burglary which had been committed recently, and so far the "gang"— as the newspapers assumed and the police believed the offenders to be—had not been caught.

Fred Mathews now thought he had every reason to believe that the same hand had executed all three crimes and that the recklessness of the last—the almost Wanton defiance of perfectly natural means of precaution and concealment—had led to the discovery of this burglar in high life.

After long deliberation, however, the young prosecutor made up his mind that he would so far compromise with his conscience as to make a personal, private call upon the young man who was under suspicion and boldly accuse him of the theft of the tell-tale cloak that had been traced to him, and take the consequences.

He was well aware that in case this course should lead to the escape of the criminal he would be compelled to bear the abuse and suspicion which would surely follow, for the evidence had passed through other hands than his own.

He knew that he was taking a method which would be called in question, and that he would not take it if the suspected man lived in a less fashionable street or had the misfortune to be low born.

All this he knew quite well, and still he argued to himself that it was the right thing for him to do, or at least that it was the best possible under the circumstances, and that after giving Walter Banks a private chance to clear himself—if such a thing were possible—he would still be in a position to go on with the case, if that should be necessary.

That night, for the first time in his career, he allowed himself to be kept awake, not by the fear that he should fail through inexperience in his duty to his client—as had happened sometimes to trouble him earlier in his professional life—but by a dread that he should wilfully betray his trust to the public. At two o'clock he lay staring at the wall, asking himself if he was becoming corrupt; if he, too, believed in shielding guilt if only that guilt were dressed in purple and spoke with a soft and cultured accent.

II.

"Mr. Banks will be down in a moment;" the trim maid had said, and left the library door open as she withdrew.

The young prosecutor walked about the room uneasily. He had hoped at the last moment that the object of his call would be from home—that he would take fright and refuse to be seen—that action had been taken by the police which would put it out of his power to give the warning that he now felt he was here to give. But, no. "Mr. Banks will be down in a moment." He had heard quite distinctly, and there had not been the slightest accent of fear or annoyance in the voice that spoke.

In his agitation he had taken up a curiously wrought paper knife which lay upon the table and had dropped it as if it had burned his fingers.

"Good God!" he exclaimed. "*He* was the college thief. It is no new thing, then."

He took up the knife again and examined it closely. There could be no mistake. It was a gold wrought, elaborately engraved blade, set in a handle which had no duplicate, for the students, who had planned the gift which had so mysteriously disappeared had devised and caused to be engraved a secret symbol which was cut deep in the polished surface.

It was to have been a surprise for one of the favorites in the faculty. It had disappeared—and here it was!

"Good morning, Mathews. This is really very kind. I—"

It was the voice of Walter Banks, but their eyes met over the fallen paper knife, which had dropped from trembling fingers at the first word.

A great wave of color rushed into the face of young Banks. The prosecutor stood mute and pale. Involuntarily he had tried to cover the knife with a corner of the rug as he turned to meet his host. It vaguely dawned upon him that he was a guest in a house where he was playing the part of a detective. His hand was extended in the hearty western fashion which had become second nature to him, but Walter Banks did not take it.

"Will you sit down?" said the host in a tone which was hoarse, and quite unlike the frank, free voice that spoke a moment before.

As he seated himself he bent forward and took up the bit of tell-tale gold and ivory. Then he said, slowly in a tone that was scarcely audible:

"Yes, I took it. You are right. It *is* the college knife."

"Don't! don't!" exclaimed Fred Mathews, rising. "I am— You forget— I am— My office. Think. I am for the prosecution!" His face was livid. Young Banks leaned heavily against the table. The color began to die out of his lips. His hand trembled as he laid the knife upon the table. Neither spoke. The brain of the young prosecutor found only scraps and shreds of thought, in which such words as duty, honor, pity, hospitality, wealth, social order, floated vaguely here and there, buffeted by the one insistent idea that he should go—go quickly—and leave this man alone with his shame and humiliation.

Walter Banks was the first to speak.

"Come up to my room. Mother might come in here and—I suppose—you have come about— I—Is—? You say you are for the prosecution. Have they traced the cloak to me?"

The lawyer stepped back again and looked at the man before him. What could he mean by saying such a thing as that—*to him?* They had never been close friends, but now in spite of everything the thought that he was the prosecutor kept itself steadily in the attorney's mind and struggled with a pity and reluctance that were seeking to justify him by a belief in the insanity of young Banks.

No one but a lunatic would have made that last remark. The thought was a relief. He grasped at it eagerly and began to fashion his mental outlook to fit the idea. Then suddenly came to him with overwhelming force all he had ever heard or read of the failure of justice where criminals of high degree were concerned.

He had followed his host to the stairs. Suddenly he turned, caught up his hat from the stand where he had left it, and passed out of the street door without a word. Once in the street he glanced involuntarily up at the house. At the window of the room he had just left stood Walter Banks. His arm was about his mother's shoulders, and both were very pale. There was a strange likeness between them.

III.

Every conceivable form of pressure to prevent the trial of Walter Banks was brought to bear in the next few weeks; but Prosecutor Mathews had pushed the case vigorously in spite of it all. He felt not only that justice was at stake, but that his own moral fibre was in pawn, as well. He held aloof from his social friends—who were in many cases the friends of the accused, also—lest he lose sight of his duty through some fresh or new form of attack upon his integrity of purpose.

It had come to his knowledge that even the Judge who was to sit in the case had been approached by the friends of the defendant, and it was felt that it would be difficult to impanel a jury that would or could be fair and impartial.

If but one man was drawn from the "upper class," the jury would be sure to hang. On the other hand, if all of the talesmen were chosen from that social caste which feels that it is usually the victim, it would go hard with Walter Banks even if he were able—as seemed wholly unlikely—to show a reasonably clear case in his favor.

The day came. The court-room held an unusual audience. There were many ladies present who had never before seen the inside of such a room. They held their breath and were filled with awe and fear—of they knew not what.

Perhaps few men can realize what it is to a woman to face for the first time the embodiment of all that her strong faith and utter ignorance has carried to mature years as an ideal of justice and dignity—of solemn obligation and fearful responsibility. To her there has been no reverse side to the picture. She believes in courts as courts of justice. She knows nothing of quibble, of technicality, of precedent. Nothing here is light or humorous to her. Next to a death chamber the criminal court-room is fullest of the thoughts which reach beyond mere human responsibility and import, and all that passes there is freighted for her with a sense of finality that few men can comprehend. *They* think of reversal of judgment.

The fiat of the court is the closing knell to a woman; and although she may know the judge in private life to be a fallible or—more incongruous still—a jovial man, his presence *here* is overpowering. Of the jury she feels vaguely, dread. Of the judge, awe.

The mother of the prisoner sat near him. Her sad, pale, refined face troubled the young prosecutor sorely and he tugged at his conscience and spurred on his resolution after each glance at her.

The case was so plain, the evidence so clear, the defence so weak that the whole tide of public sentiment swung rapidly from the side of the prisoner to that of the people.

The indignation for him which had been felt by the society women who had come to show themselves as his friends changed into scorn and contempt. The whole mental atmosphere of the room underwent a revolution. When court opened few besides the officers believed him guilty. As the case drew near its close no one believed him innocent. He had not been allowed by his counsel to take the stand in his own behalf, and this had told strongly against him in the minds of both jury and spectators. The prosecuting attorney had made a telling speech, and the charge of the judge was plainly indicative of his opinion that there was but one verdict to give.

The jury had taken but one ballot. They had needed no charge from the judge at all.

"Guilty,"—came from the foreman's lips with a decided accent that indicated a certain satisfaction in pronouncing it. The prisoner's face grew a shade paler, but the puzzled light in his eyes lost nothing of that weary, insistent questioning that had marked their depths all day. Indeed, he seemed to be as much surprised, as the evidence had been unfolded, as were the friends who were there to see him vindicated.

During the speech of the prosecutor and the charge of the judge young Banks; mother had held her son's hand and tears had dropped unheeded from her eyes.

The judge had spoken again, but no one moved. The attorney for the prisoner bent forward and touched him on the shoulder.

"Stand up for sentence," he said. "The judge"—

"Sit still!" It was the woman beside him who spoke. She had dried her tears. Every face in the room was turned toward her now. She staggered to her feet. Her voice penetrated every corner of the room.

"*I* am the thief, judge. Sentence me. I stole the cloak!"

"Mother, mother! Great God, it is not true! Mother, sit down! She never saw the coat. Mother! Mother! Great God, what does it mean?"

The young fellow had sprung to his feet, but she eluded his grasp, and before any one knew what she intended to do she passed onto the witness stand.

There was a tense silence in the room. No one was prepared for the scene. It had been so swiftly done—so wholly without warning—that every one sat dumb.

She had caught up the Bible as she reached the stand and pressed it to her lips. She was vaguely aware that this act was looked upon as affecting the credibility of the witness. She also imagined that it gave her a right to put in her evidence even at this stage of the trial. She supposed that a trial was for the purpose of arriving at the facts and that the Court sat with that object alone in view. She did not know that it was too late. She was unaware that the case would have to be reopened to admit her evidence. She did not know that it was possible for the gate of justice to be swung shut in the face of truth. She supposed that all trials were for the one purpose of getting at the bottom of the case; so that it did not occur to her that her action was strange only in so far as such a confession from such a woman must be so regarded by all who knew her, and who was there in all the town who did not know and respect her?

The young prosecutor sat mute. The eyes of the judge widened in astonishment. For the moment he was the man and neighbor only. He forgot his office. She was talking rapidly, and all were listening.

"I am the thief, judge. Let me tell you. It is not right that he should suffer for my crime. Poor boy, his life has been a hell on earth for *me—for me!* And he has never understood. I could not tell him. I shall now. He shall understand. *You* shall, judge. Oh, God, if only a woman sat where you do—a mother! But let me tell you; I can. I thought I could not; but I can—even to *these* gentlemen." She waved her hand toward the jury and there was a widening of her nostrils as if her breath and courage were leaving her. "Rather than have him punished, disgraced, ruined, I can tell it all. He is *not* guilty. It is I! It is I!" She put her trembling hands to her temples and her eyes were those of a hunted creature at bay.

"Before he came into the world—you'll let me tell you frankly, judge? *I must.* Before he came into the world I made him what he is—a thief. Did I or did his father? It was like this. I am ashamed to tell it, but, oh, judge, I *loved* him, and I longed to make the pretty things and buy the dainty ones that would make his soft, white, dimpled flesh look sweeter when he should lie before me. His father was—you knew his father, judge. He was a good man, but— You know how he loved money—and power. He— I— I was the pauper most young wives are. I was too proud to ask for money, and if I *had* asked often— But I was too proud, so, perhaps, I need not tell about the if. Most women know it, and— You could not understand."

She paused. A panic had overtaken her nerves. She was becoming vaguely conscious of her position. Her eyes wandered over the room; but when they fell upon her son, sitting with his wretched face pinched and startled, with his deep eyes staring at her, her courage came again.

"At first I had no thought of theft. I used to go each night after my husband fell asleep and take a little money from his pocket. Only a little. He never missed it—never. So he used to whip the boy for stealing afterward and said he would disgrace us and— I never told him even then. Life was horrible. The growing certainty maddened me. He would steal anything, everything about the house, even his own things. He did not understand himself and he could not help it; but I did not think it would ever come to *this*—through me—*through me!*"

She calmed herself again suddenly by a glance at her son.

"Every night I took only a little money. My motive was a good one. I knew my husband did not understand how I longed to get the pretty things. How— Of course in one sense I had a right to the money. He was rich even then, but—I *felt* myself a—pauper—and a thief.

"I— Do you think young mothers should be young paupers, judge? I've sometimes thought that if they were not there might be less use for courts like this—and prisons.

"I've sometimes thought if mothers sat on juries they'd know the reasons why for crime and wrong and, maybe, work to cure the causes of the crimes rather than simply punish those who have committed them blindly—*often blindly.*

"I've sometimes thought the cost—in money—would be less; and then the cost in love and sorrow! Oh, judge, be patient just a little longer. Do not let them stop me. It means so much to *us!* I'll go back to the point. I'll tell the truth—all of it—all. But it is hard to do it—here.

"I bought the little wardrobe; but remember, judge, the months and months of daily building, bone on bone, fibre within fibre, thought on thought that is moulded into shape for human beings!

"I knew your father, judge. Your eyes are like his, but all your mental life— your temperament—you got from other blood than filled his veins.

"Your father's mother gave you your character. Your gentle heart is hers— your patient thoughtfulness. I knew her well. I knew your mother, too. She was the teacher of my motherhood. It was to her I told the truth in my boy's childhood—when I first began to realize or fear what I had done. You owe it all to her that you are strong and true. She understood in time—and now you sit in judgment on my boy, whose mother learned from yours too late the meaning and the danger of it all. She saved my other children. I killed my pride for them. *I asked for money.* The others may be *beggars* some day—they never will be thieves.

"That boy has never asked a favor. He simply cannot. His pride was always stronger than anything—anything except his love for me.

"I knit that in his blood too. I loved him so I made myself a thief for him. Of course I did not know—I did not understand the awful danger then; but— A young mother—I—it is hard to tell it here. You will not understand—you cannot. Oh, God, for a mother on the jury! A mother on the bench!"

She caught at her escaping courage again. The officer whose duty it was to take her away moved forward a second time, and a second time the judge motioned him back. She had been his mother's friend ever since he could remember, and the ordinary discipline of the court was not for her. He would do his duty, he said to himself, but surely there was no haste. All this was irregular, of course, but if something should come of it that gave excuse for a new trial no one would be more thankful than he.

"Young mothers are so ignorant. They know so little of all the things of which they should know much. They are so helpless. Judge, there will be criminal courts and prisons—oh, so many of both—just as long as motherhood is ignorant and helpless and swayed by feeling only. Don't you know it is ignorance and feeling that leads to crime? If people only understood! If only they were able to think it out to what it means, crimes would not be—but they cannot, they cannot! Those trembling lips you see before you are no more truly a copy of mine—the boy is as responsible for the set and curve of those lips—as he is for his hopeless fault. He has stolen from his infancy; but I, not he, am the thief. Now sentence the real criminal, judge. Courts are to punish the guilty—not to further curse the helpless victims. I am the criminal here. Sentence me!"

"Mother! Mother! I never understood my-self before! Oh, mother, mother!"

It was a wild cry from Walter Banks as his mother had risen asking for sentence on herself. He sprang forward, forgetting everything and took her in his arms. There was a great stir in the room.

"Silence in the court!"

Mrs. Banks had fainted. Her son helped to carry her into another room. No one attempted to prevent him. The young prosecutor returned with him and stood dumb before the court.

"I am ready for sentence, your Honor. I committed the burglary." It was the voice of the prisoner. He was standing with his arms folded and his eyes cast down. Silence fell in the room. The women ceased to sob. There was an uneasy movement in the jury box.

"In view of the new evidence—" began the foreman but the voice of the judge, slow and steady, filled the room.

"It is the sentence of this court that you, Walter Banks, be confined at hard labor in the state penitentiary for the term of four years."

The prisoner bowed and turned a shade paler.

"Do not tell mother that until she is better," he said to his attorney and passed out in the custody of the sheriff.

"And at the end of four years, what!" a lady was saying to the young prosecutor as the room slowly emptied.

"The brute!" was hurled after the judge by another, as his form vanished through the door.

"Shows that law is not for the poor alone—"

"Good things for social order and—"

"Well, yes, I'm rather disappointed; but of course a judge can't go behind the returns."

"Evidence all one way if—"

"Heavens, what a scene!"

"—my opinion no woman should ever be admitted to a court room except as a prisoner. It—"

"Feather in the cap of the prosecutor."

"—re-election sure enough now."

"Whole thing in a nutshell—"

"Simple question. *Did* he commit the burglary? If so—"

The young prosecutor hurried away from the sound of these voices and the congratulations of his political friends. He was mentally sore and perplexed because he had won his case.

That night he called upon the prisoner for the second time.

"I have made up' my mind to resign my office," he said, not looking at the convict, who had risen to receive him.

Walter Banks was by far the calmer of the two, but he did not speak.

"I shall never be able to act for the prosecution again. I thought this case was so clear. My duty seemed so plain—too plain to admit of anything but the most vigorous course of action; but—"

"You did nothing but your duty, Mathews. We are all victims I suppose— one way or another. You are going to be the victim of your sensitive conscience. The result will be a course of vacillation that will ruin your chances of success. I am sorry. You've got all the elements for a leader—only you've got a conscience. That settles it. A bit of heredity like that is as fatal as—as mine." He bit his lips.

"Don't let your part in my case worry you. The game of life has gone against me. That is all. The dice were loaded before I ever got hold of them. I did what I could to out-live—out-fight my awful—inheritance. I wasn't strong enough. It got the best of me. Nature is a terrible antagonist. Perhaps now that I understand myself better I shall be able to keep a firmer hold. You did your duty, Mathews; good-by. Be— Can't you be a little kind to mother? She suffers so. Her punishment is double—and her crime was ignorance!"

This time he took the hand that was held out to him.

"Only ignorance," he added. "It seems an awful punishment for that."

"Ignorance—and poverty and love," said the young prosecutor as the door closed behind him, "and Nature did the rest! What a grip is at our throats! And how we help blind Nature in her cruel work by laws and customs and conditions! What a little way we've come from barbarism yet! How slow we travel. But we are moving," he added with a deep sigh. "Moving a little. There is light ahead. If not for us, then for those who come after."

He heard the bolt slip behind him and shuddered.

"It might as easily have been I," he mused as he went down the steps, and shuddered again.

"I doubt if it was fault of his or virtue of mine that determined which of us two should be the prosecutor."

A RUSTY LINK IN THE CHAIN.

"In the brainy that wondrous world with one inhabitant, there are recesses dim and dark, treacherous sands and dangerous shores, where seeming sirens tempt and fade; streams that rise in unknown lands from hidden springs, strange seas with ebb and flow of tides, resistless billows urged by storms of flame, profound and awful depths hidden by mist of dreams, obscure and phantom realms where vague and fearful things are half revealed, jungles where passion's tigers crouch, and skies of cloud and hue where fancies fly with painted wings that dazzle and mislead; and the poor sovereign of this pictured world is led by old desires and ancient hates, and stained by crimes of many vanished years, and pushed by hands that long ago were dust, until he feels like some bewildered slave that Mockery has throned and crowned."

Ingersoll.

When I called, last Sunday afternoon, as was my habit, upon my old college friend—now a distinguished physician—I found him sitting in his office holding in his hand a letter. His manner was unusually grave and, I thought, troubled. I asked him, laughingly, if he had had bad news from beyond the seas—from his Castle in Spain.

"No, it is worse than that, I fear," he said gravely. "It looks to me very much like bad news from beyond the grave—from the Castle of Heredity in the realm of an Ancestor."

"I hope, doctor, that you have not had,—that my little jest was not a cruel touch upon a real hurt."

"Not at all, not at all, old fellow," he said, smiling a little.

"It is not my own trouble at all; but—well, it set me to thinking strange thoughts. Shall I tell you about it? I should really like to know just how it would impress you—an intelligent man out of the profession."

He placed the letter on the table beside him, looked at me steadily for a moment, and then began:

"It may be as well to say that I have never before ventured to tell the story of George Wetherell's curious experience, simply because I have always felt certain that to a really intelligent and well-in-formed physician it would be a comparatively familiar, and not specially startling (although a wholly uncomprehended) phase of human disorder; while to many, not of the profession, it would appear to involve such fearful and far-reaching results, that they would either refuse to believe it possible at all, or else jump to the conclusion that numerous cases which have only some slight point of similarity are to be classed with it and explained upon the same basis.

"In regard to these latter persons, I do not intend to convey the impression that I am either ambitious to shield them from the consequences of their own nimble and unguarded reckonings, or that by my silence in this particular instance I suppose that I have prevented them from forming quite as erroneous opinions founded upon some other equally misunderstood and ill-digested scrap of psychological and medical information.

"But it has sometimes seemed to me that there were certain features connected with the case of George Wetherell which, in the hands of the ignorant or unscrupulous, might easily be used to the disadvantage of their fellow-beings, and I have therefore hesitated to lay it before any one who was not, in my opinion, both intelligent and honorable enough to accept it as one of the strange manifestations in an individual experience; and to understand, because of the innumerable conditions of mental and physical heredity— which were not likely ever to occur again in the same proportions—that therefore the same manifestations were, not to be looked for in a sufficient number of persons to ever make this case in any sense a type or a guide.

"Notwithstanding this, there are, as I said in the first place, certain features connected with it which many members of the medical profession will recognize; but they are none the less puzzling symptoms.

"The matter has been brought back with unusual force to my mind at this time, by a circumstance connected with one of Wetherell's children, which is detailed in this letter. It lends a new touch of interest to the malady of the father. To enable you to obtain even a fairly comprehensive idea of the strange development, it will be necessary for me to tell you, first, something about the man and his surroundings.

"To be as brief as I may, then, he was the son of a merry, whole-souled, stout, and, withal, mentally alert, Southern gentleman, who had taken the law into his own hands and duly scandalized the reputable part of the community in which he lived by giving his slaves (all of whom he or his wife had inherited) their freedom at a time and under circumstances which made it necessary for him to betake himself with some considerable alacrity to a part of the country where it was looked upon as respectable to pay for the voluntary services of one's fellowmen, rather than to pay for the man himself with the expectation that the services were to be thrown in.

"Of course it was imperative—not only for the peace, but for the safety of all parties concerned—for him to transport both his family and his freed-men to a place where it was at once honorable for a white man to do such a deed and for a black man to own himself. This he did; and while a number of the negroes remained in the service of the family, the son (on whose account, and to prevent whom from believing in and being enervated by the possession of slaves the step had, in great measure, been taken) had grown to manhood with a curious mingling of Southern sympathies and Northern reasoning and convictions.

"The outbreak of the war found the young fellow struggling bravely, with all the fire and energy of a peculiarly gifted nature, to establish a newspaper in a border State, and to convince his readers that the extension of slavery would be a grave calamity, not only for the owned but for the owner.

"His two associates were Eastern college-bred men, and it was therefore deemed wisest to push young Wetherell forward as the special champion of free soil, under the illusion that his Southern birth and sympathies would win for him a more ready and kindly hearing on a subject which at that time was a dangerous one to handle freely, especially in the border-land then under dispute.

"But the three young enthusiasts had reckoned, as young people will, upon a certain degree of reason about, and calm discussion of, a question which at that time they still recognized as having two very strong and serious sides; for they had not taken the stand of the Abolition party at all. They called themselves free-soil Democrats, and were simply arguing against the extension of an institution which they were not yet prepared to believe it wise to attempt to abolish where it was already established, and where there was seemingly no other peaceable or fair solution than the one of limitation and gradual emancipation, through the process of mental and moral development of the ruling race. This position was not an unnatural one, surely, for young Wetherell, and was only what might have been expected from the son of a man who had given practical demonstration of the possibility of such evolution in the slave-holding and slave-dependent class.

"But, as I have intimated, the confidence and reasonableness of youth had led to a complete misconception as to the temper of the opposition. It is quite possible that the frank, passionate, free-soil editorials, if they had come from either of the Eastern men, might have been accepted as the delusions of youth, the prejudice of section, or, at worst, as the arguments of partisans; but from a man of Southern birth—the son of a law-breaker (you must remember that the enfranchisement of the slaves had been a serious infraction of the law, strange as that sounds to the ears of the present generation)—from the son of such a man they could mean only a malicious desire to stir up strife and cause bloodshed by making restless slaves dangerous and dangerous slaves desperate. The result was that one night, after the issue of a paper containing an article of unusual force and power, young Wetherell found himself startled from a sound sleep, in the back room of his office, by the smell of smoke and gleam of flame.

"He understood their significance at a glance, and knew that escape by the front door meant a reception by masked men, five minutes for prayer, and—a rope.

"Springing from the back window into the river, he swam to the other shore, and within a few days raised the first regiment of volunteers that the State sent in response to the call of the President, and cut adrift at once and forever from all effort to argue the case from an ethical or a financial outlook.

"It is more than likely that anger may have had something to do with his sudden conversion from a 'peace and argument,' to first a 'war Democrat,' and shortly thereafter to a Republican; but be that as it may, it is certain that at such crises as these, mental activity is spurred and radical changes are made with a rapidity and decision astonishing to contemplate in periods of quiet and peace.

"So it came about that this lad of twenty-three suddenly found himself at the head of a regiment of somewhat desperate border men, most of whom were more than twice his own age, wildly charging a battery in one of the first battles of the war.

"He received three wounds, one of which was a slight abrasion of the scalp, not looked upon as more than a scratch by either the surgeon or himself; indeed, it would hardly be worth mentioning but for the strange events which followed. Whether this wound had anything to do with the condition of which I am about to tell, you will have to decide for yourself; but I must warn you, in the beginning, that there was nothing like a fracture of the skull, and the little path made by the bullet through the scalp healed without trouble, almost without attention, and never afterward gave the slightest pain.

"The hair, it is true, did not grow again over the parting, and, as it was nearly in the middle of his head, it made him an involuntary follower of the fashion of a certain effeminate type of youths for whom he had an overwhelming contempt. Neither of the other two wounds was serious, and after a very short period in the hospital he reported for duty, was promoted, and given sole charge of a post of considerable importance.

"Shortly thereafter his father received a some what discomposing telegram. He had previously had several more or less lucid despatches from his son while the patient was still in the hospital; but any lack of clearness in their wording had been attributed to haste or to carelessness in the transmission, and as they all indicated rapid recovery, no undue anxiety had been felt. But the message in question now produced the impression that there was something wrong. It read: 'Send me one thousand swords immediately.'

"After a few moments' consultation with the boy's mother, Mr. Wetherell packed his hand-bag, and, armed with a letter from President Lincoln, whose personal friend he was, started for the seat of war.

"Upon arriving at his destination, the son expressed no surprise whatever, but much pleasure, at seeing his father. He asked, in the most natural and affectionate way, about each member of the family, and then suddenly put his hand to his head and appeared to be in deep thought.

"His eyes contracted in the manner peculiar to some persons when attempting to recall a long-forgotten event; but in a moment this had passed away and he appeared to be perfectly clear and natural.

"He attended to the affairs of his office in a manner which not only escaped criticism, but won praise from his superiors, and conversed with great freedom and marked intelligence on the stirring subjects of the time.

"He had had some little fever while his wounds were fresh, but in no degree to cause alarm, and even this had now almost entirely left him. In short, he appeared to be in nearly perfect mental and physical health. There was, however, one peculiarity which the father noticed as unfamiliar in his son; but as it was not at all strange that so young a man—or any man, indeed, who had suddenly been given control of matters of such grave importance— should at times be very quiet and appear to be struggling to recall some matter of moment, the habit was not given more than passing attention, and it was not sufficiently marked to be noticed at all by any one except a near relation. At these times young Wetherell would contract his eyebrows, look steadily at some object near him,—as the toe of his boot or the palm of his hand,— raise his head suddenly, gaze at the distant horizon, bite his lip, and then appear to either give it up or be satisfied with some mental solution of his puzzle.

"One day his father said: 'What is it, George?'

"The young fellow turned his eyes quickly upon his father and asked:

"'Have I forgotten anything? It seems to me there is something I just fail to recall. I am on the edge of it constantly, but it slips. I can't get quite enough hold on it to be sure what it is—or to be certain, indeed, that it is anything. Can you think of anything I ought to do that I have overlooked?'

"This all sounded natural enough, and was, seemingly, a condition not unfamiliar to his father, so they began together going over the duties pertaining to the son's office to see if, by a mischance, something had been neglected. Everything was complete and in perfect order; but still the look returned from time to time, until it became almost habitual.

"This was ten days after his father had reached camp, and his plan was to leave for home that afternoon; for, as I said, the boy's wounds were almost entirely healed, and he appeared to be in need of nothing whatever. More and more his superior officers called him into their councils, and more and more his clear judgment was commended by them.

"He was to walk to the train with his father. The moment they were outside the limits of the camp George remarked, casually, 'I must stop on the way and order those swords.'

"The remark recalled the queer telegram which had caused Mr. Wetherell to come to his son, the wording of which had been wholly obliterated from his mind by their meeting.

"'What swords?' inquired his father, now on the alert again.

"The young fellow turned and looked at his father for a moment, and then said: 'I don't know. It is a secret order. Don't mention it. The general told me to order them. They are to be sent to me.'

"This all seemed probable enough to Mr. Wetherell, and yet he somehow felt, rather than saw, a queer change in his son's eyes, which he thought he had noticed once or twice before.

"He decided not to return home for the present.

"When he told his son this, the boy took it quite as a matter of course, and made no comment whatever on the sudden alteration of purpose.

"On the way back to camp George stepped into a military supply station and ordered fourteen hundred swords to be delivered to him immediately.

"By this time his father had made up his mind that there were short intervals in which the young colonel did not know exactly what he was doing—or, rather, that while he did know and act intelligently—from the outlook of the moment—it was a time wholly disconnected from the rest of his life, and when the moment was past he had no farther recollection of it.

"However, Mr. Wetherell was not sure enough of this to risk compromising a probably brilliant future by a premature or unnecessarily public announcement, and he therefore allowed the order to be made, and taken in good faith, and walked back to camp with his son, who immediately went about his duties in the most intelligent and scrupulously careful manner.

"Mr. Wetherell, however, made a call upon the officer in command the moment he could do so without attracting attention; and after a long talk (in which the secret sword order was discovered to be a delusion), it was decided that the recently recovered invalid should retire from the field on the sick leave, which he had previously refused to consider.

"When he was told of this arrangement, he agreed to it without a murmur, and began, for the first time for many days, to have his wounds (which were now past the need of it) dressed with much care. This he continued every morning, but by the time they reached home he had become possessed with the belief that his chief wound was in his side, where there had not been a scratch.

"To humor him, the family physician applied bandages to the imaginary injury every day regularly.

"All this time there was no clearer talker, no more acute reasoner, no more simple, earnest, gentlemanly fellow to be found than Col. George Wetherell, whom his townsmen were honoring and inducing to make public speeches and write clear, firm, inspiring editorials for one of the leading papers. No one except his own family and physician suspected for a moment that he was not mentally as bright as he always had been, and even the younger members of the family were without the least hint of it.

"Indeed, his father and the doctor both thought that his only illusion now was a belief in the wound in his side. Several weeks passed, and even this indication was losing its force, for he no longer required medical attention, and was as well and as rational as ever in his life, so far as any one could perceive, when one day a stranger appeared and asked for him. Mr. Wetherell requested the gentleman (who was evidently laboring under great excitement) to be seated, and at the same time made up his own mind to be present during the interview.

"Colonel Wetherell was summoned, and, on entering the room, looked in a startled way at the stranger, smiled vaguely, extended his hand, contracted his eyes into a long, narrow line, turned white, and throwing both arms suddenly above his head, exclaimed: 'My God! my God! what have I done? Where am I? How long has it been? Is she dead? Is she dead?' and staggered back into his father's arms.

"His distress was so manifest, that the visitor lost his severity at once, and said quite gently: 'No, she is not dead; but she is almost insane with fright, and has been so exhausted with anxiety and tears, that we had lost all hope for her reason, or even for her life, unless I could find you. I have been through the lines, was delayed by the loss of my passport, and it is now five weeks since I saw her. She is alive, but—'

"Young Wetherell sprang to his feet, and turned on his father like a madman. 'How dared you?' he demanded; 'how dared you keep back my letters? You have killed her. You have murdered her, poor, delicate girl, with anxiety and doubt of me.' And then with set teeth and white lips he advanced upon his father, his arm uplifted, as if he held a sword, and with a sweep which would have severed chords of steel, if the weapon had really been within his grasp, he brought his arm across his father's breast and sank upon the floor, senseless and still.

"Afterward, when he revived, he had no recollection of what had occurred, except alone the fact that for many weeks previous he had forgotten utterly the girl who was to be his wife, whose life and love were all his world. While he had remembered everything else, had carefully attended to the smallest details of daily life, the link of memory that held the fact of her existence had been coated with a rust of absolute oblivion. The single link in all the chain of memory that had failed him had been the one the nearest to his heart— the dearest one of all!

"They were married two months later, and he resumed command of his regiment. Through an honorable and eventful life no sign of mental lapse ever returned; but every day he dreaded it, and watched his wife and children as a man might do who saw a creeping monster back of those he loved while he stood paralyzed and dumb. He never seemed to fear that other things might lose their hold upon his consciousness; but the apprehension that his mind would slip the link which held his wife, and leave her sick and faint with anxious fears, which he alone could still, constantly haunted him.

"His wounds never troubled him again. He died not long ago. His career was an exceptionally brilliant one. You would know him if I had given his real name, for it was in the public ear for years.

"There were but six persons who ever knew the history of his case, and they are still unable to explain it—its cause, its direction, its cure. Or is it cured? Will his children be subject to it? Will it take the same form? Was it caused by the wound? by the fever? Or were hereditary conditions so grouped as to produce this mental effect, even if there had been no wound—no illness? If the latter, will it be transmitted? These questions come to me with renewed force, to-day, as I hold in my hand this letter, asking me to give the family history of Col. George Wetherell for the use of physicians in a distant city who are now treating his son. This son has reached the precise age at which his father had the strange experience of which I have just told you.

"There is a hint in the letter which, in the light of the father's malady, appears to a physician to be of peculiar importance from a medical outlook.

"We shall see, we shall see."

There was a long pause; then he asked: "Should you, a layman, look to the wound to explain the condition? Or to the Castle of Heredity? Suppose the son's malady is quite similar—as now appears—what then?"

THE BOLER HOUSE MYSTERY.

"What would you do? what would you say now, if you were in such a position?"—
Thackeray.

*"Thackeray is always protesting that no good is to be done by blinking the truth. Let us
have facts out, and mend what is bad if we can"*—Trollope.

Mr. John Boler had been in the hotel business, as he phrased it, ever since he
was born. Before he could walk he had been the "feature" of his father's
summer hotel, where he was the only baby to be passed around and hugged
into semi-unconsciousness by all the women in the house. Because of the
scarcity of his kind, too, he was subjected to untold agony by the male guests,
most of whom appeared to believe that the chief desire of his infantile heart
was to be tossed skyward from hour to hour and caught in upstretched hands
as he descended with a sickening sense of insecurity and a wild hysterical
laugh. In these later years he often said that he would like to know who those
summer fiends were who had made his infancy so full of narrow escapes
from sudden and violent death. Finally he thought he had revenge at hand.
A benevolent-looking old gentleman came puffing up to the desk of the
Boler House, and, after registering, proceeded to question the genial
proprietor as to his identity.

"Dear me, dear me," he puffed, "and so you are the son of old John Boler,
the best hotel-keeper the sun ever shone upon! Why, I remember tossing you
up to the rafters under the porch of your father's house when you were only
the size of a baked apple and mighty nigh as measly looking. Well, well, to be
sure you had grit for a young one. Never got scared. Always yelled for more.
I believe if you had batted your soft little head against the roof you'd have
laughed all the louder and kicked until you did it again," and the old man
chuckled with the pleasure of age and retrospection.

"Yes, I remember well," said Mr. Boler, casting about in his own mind for
the form of revenge he should take on this man now that he was to have the
chance for which he had so longed and waited.

His first thought was to put him in the room next to the three sporting men
who played poker and told questionable stories of their own exploits after
two o'clock every night, but that hardly seemed adequate. The room
adjoining the elevator popped into his head. Every time the old gentleman
fell asleep *bang* would go that elevator door or *bzzzz* would start off the bell
so suddenly that it would leave him unnerved and frantic in the morning. But
what was that? What John Boler yearned for was to make the punishment fit
the crime, and, after all these years of planning and wishing for the chance,

here it was, and he felt that he could think of nothing, absolutely nothing, bad enough.

So with a fine satire which was wholly lost upon his victim, Mr. Boler ordered him taken to the very best room in the house, and made up his mind that after disarming all suspicion in that way he would set about his revenge, which should take some exquisitely torturous form.

All this had run through his mind with great rapidity while the old gentleman talked. Then Mr. Boler turned the register around, wrote "98" opposite the name. Said he should be delighted to show his own mettle to one of his father's old guests, called out "Front," and transferred his attention to a sweet-faced girl who stood waiting her turn to register.

"A small room, please," she said in a voice scarcely above a whisper. Mr. Boler knew just what it meant in an instant. He knew that she was not used to hotels—that she was uncertain what to do, and that she wanted her living to cost her as little as possible. She was evidently a lady, and quite as evidently from some small town.

"Front," he called again. "Show this lady to 96. Step lively." Front grinned. Ninety-six was a mere closet with no window except one facing a dark shaft. Indeed, it had once been the dressing-room and clothes press for the adjoining suite, and so far as Front could remember had never been used as a sleeping apartment by any one except the valet of a certain French gentleman who once occupied 98.

"Took my revenge on the wrong person that time," mused Mr. Boler as he saw the lady enter the elevator. "Now I wonder why I did that?" But Mr. John Boler had his little superstition, as most of us have, and whenever he was moved by a perfectly blind impulse to do a thing, he always believed that "something would come of it sure," as he expressed it. "Never knew it to fail. Of course I don't believe in such things; but—" and then he would laugh and go on believing in it as implicitly as ever.

All day he brooded over what he should do to old Winkle, as he called the man in 98, and as surely as his mind grew exhausted and his various plans fell through, his thoughts would catch a glimpse of the timid girl in the next room, and he would smilingly wink to himself and say, "Something will come of it, something will come of it sure. Never put a guest in that beastly room before, and I had nothing against *her*. *Must* have been him It was after." He always called his blind impulses "It" when he was utilizing them for superstitious purposes or to quiet his reason.

"I'll bet that girl being in that closet will be the means of getting me even with old Winkle yet, and she is not used to city hotels. She'll think that it is all right

- 64 -

and she will most likely be out all day. It's not so bad to sleep in after all. Quietest room in the house."

The next morning Mr. Winkle strolled into the office and harassed Mr. Boler about his infancy, reminding him that he had possessed a very weak stomach. "And who wouldn't," thought that gentleman indignantly, "if he was pitched about like a bale of hay from morning till night by every fool that got hold of him?" but he smiled pleasantly and said no doubt he had been very much like other infants, judging from the way he grew up. He looked upon a baby as the embryonic man, and as he was about an average adult male biped now, he had most likely been very close to an average male infant. "I might have been more," he hinted darkly, "but for certain idiotic people," and then he laughed. For it was not in Mr. John Boler's nature to be openly unpleasant to any one. This was the secret of his success as an innkeeper.

"By the way, Johnnie," said old Mr. Winkle late the next afternoon, "I thought I heard some one sobbing in the room next to mine last night. This morning I concluded I was mistaken, but now I'm sure I heard it. Anybody sick in there? I tried the door that leads into my room but it was locked. It sounds like a woman's voice. It always did tear the very heart out of me to hear a woman cry—" He went on talking but Mr. John Boler heard no more. His heart gave a wild bound of delight. "It" had given him his revenge. He would let the young woman stay in the hotel free of charge as long as old Winkle was in the house if only she would weep and sob pretty steadily. "'Johnnie,' by gad," thought he, resenting this new indignity to his name. "By George, what luck!" And then he went about his duties with a new spring in his always elastic step. At the lunch hour the following day he glanced into the dining-room, and sure enough, there sat the occupant of 96, and her eyes were swollen and red. At almost any other time this would have disturbed John Boler, but now it was a deep delight to him.

"Had a spat with her lover, no doubt," speculated he, "and, by Jove! it came at a lucky time for me. I'd pay her lover to keep up the row for three weeks if I could get at him. 'Weak stomach,' 'Johnnie,' indeed!" And he went back to the office rubbing his hands in a satisfied way, thinking that old Winkle would be afraid to go to his room that night, and that his sleep would be broken by visions of a weeping woman next door, even if she did not keep him awake half the time sobbing because Ralph had called her a mean thing or a proud stuck-up flirt, and hinted darkly that she was in love with his rival.

Matters had gone on in this way for nearly a week and Mr. Winkle had fretted and fumed and asked for another room two or three times, but Mr. Boler told him that the house was full and that there wasn't another room fit to offer him anyhow. He said that he would change the young lady's room as soon as he could, but he expected her to leave every day. She went out a good deal and wrote a large number of letters, and he felt sure she was going to remain only a day or two longer. He apologized and explained and planned, and then he would chuckle to himself the moment "old Winkle's" back was turned to think how "*It*" had succeeded in getting him even with the old reprobate without the least overt act on his part.

But the eighth morning Mr. Winkle rebelled outright. He said that he would wring the girl's worthless neck if he could get at her, but he could not and would not bear her sobs any longer. The night before they had been worse than ever and he had not slept a wink all night long. At last Mr. Boler promised that he would transfer the girl to another room that very afternoon if she did not leave, and the old man softened at once and said if she could not afford to pay for any other room he would pay the difference and she need never know it.

John Boler was not mercenary, but this offer gave him keen delight. For "old Winkle" would have to buy his relief after all. He thought how willingly a certain infant of his memory would have paid for rest and quiet too when it was helpless clay in the hands of certain old imbeciles he knew of.

At 2 p.m. he told Front to go up to 96 and tell the young lady that he now had a better room for her that would cost her no more than the one she now occupied, and to change her and her belongings to 342 forthwith. In five minutes Front came back as white as a cloth and said that the young lady's door was unlocked, that there were a number of letters on the table and that she was dead.

Mr. John Boler dashed from behind the desk across the street and was back in an incredibly short space of time, dragging behind him the dignified and wealthy physician whose office faced the hotel.

At this stage of the proceedings he cautioned the employees not to say a word about the matter on pain of instant dismissal. They one and all promised, and then proceeded to tell the first reporter who dropped in that a young lady had committed suicide upstairs and that she had cried out loud for a week. They gave a full description of her and her effects, all of which appeared in the 5 o'clock edition of the paper, duly headlined with her name and certain gratuitous speculations in regard to her motive for self-destruction. In these it was darkly hinted that she was no better than she should be, but now that she was dead "we" (the immaculate young gentlemen of the press) felt disposed to draw a veil of charity over her past and say with the law that her suicide proved her insanity, and that her mental condition might also account for her past frailties.

While these generous young gentlemen were penning their reports the doctor and Mr. John Boler worked over the poor helpless body of the unconscious girl in the dark little room upstairs. Between times they read the letters on the table and learned the old, old story—not of crime, but of misfortune. No work had offered, and she must work or starve—or sell the only value she possessed in the sight of men. One or two of the answers to her advertisement had boldly hinted at this, and when her little stock of money had run out and the little stock of misfortune had swelled into a mountain, and the little pile of insults had increased until she felt that she could endure life no longer, she had concluded to brave another world where she was taught to believe a loving Father awaited her because she had been good and true and pure to the last in spite of storms and disappointments and temptations. So she made the wild leap in the dark, confident that the hereafter could hold nothing worse, and believing sincerely that it must hold something better for Her and her kind, even if that better were only forgetfulness.

Up to this point her story was that of thousands of helpless girls who face the unknown dangers of a great city with the confidence of youth, and that ill training and ignorance of the world which is supposed to be a part of the charm of young womanhood. She had not registered her real name, it is true; but this was because she intended to advertise for work and have the replies sent to the hotel, and somehow she thought that it would be easier for her to do that over a name less sacred to her than her mother's, which was also her own. So instead of registering as Fannie Ellis Worth of Atlanta, she had written "Miss Kate Jarvis" and had given no address whatever. This latter fact told strongly against her with the reporters. They located her in a certain house on Thirty-first Street and "interviewed" the madam, who gave them a picture of a girl who had once been there, and a cut of this picture appeared in two of the morning papers with the fuller account of the suicide. A beautiful moral was appended to this history of the girl's life "which had now come to its appropriate ending." But when one of these enterprising young gentlemen of the press called to get the details of the funeral for his paper, he was shocked to learn that the young lady was not dead after all, and that she was now in a fair way to recover. He was still further disgusted when neither Mr. Boler nor the attending physician would submit to an interview and declined to allow him to send his card to the girl's room.

Then and there he made up his mind that if he had to rewrite that two-column report to fit the new developments in the case, he would, as he expressed it, make John Boler and pompous Dr. Ralston wish that they had never been born. Incident to this undertaking, he would darkly hint at a number of things in regard to the girl herself and their relations with her. This was not at all to make her wish that she had never been born; but if it should serve that purpose, the young gentleman did not feel that he would be in the least to blame—if, indeed, he gave the matter a thought at all, which he very likely did not.

The article he wrote was certainly very "wide awake" and surprised even himself in its ingenuity of conjecture as to the motive which could prompt two such men as John Boler, proprietor of the Boler House, and Dr. Ralston, "whose reputation had heretofore been above suspicion, to place themselves in so unenviable, not to say dangerous, a position." He suggested that although the young woman had taken her case out of the jurisdiction of the coroner by not actually dying, this fact did not relieve the affair of certain features which demanded the prompt attention of the police court. The matter was perfectly clear. Here was a young woman who had attempted to relieve herself, by rapid means, of the life which all the social and financial conditions which surrounded her had combined to take by a slower and more painful process. If she had succeeded, the law held that she was of unsound mind—that she was, in short, a lunatic—and treated her case accordingly; but, on the other hand, if she failed, or if, as in this instance, her effort to place herself beyond want and pain was thwarted by others, then the law was equally sure that she was *not* a lunatic at all, but that she was a criminal, and that it was the plain duty of the police judge to see that she was put with those of her class—the enemies and outcasts of society.

It was also quite clear that any one who aided, abetted, or shielded a criminal was *particeps criminis*, and that unless Mr. John Boler and Dr. Ralston turned the young offender over to the police at once, there was a virtuous young reporter on the *Daily Screamer* who intended to know the reason why.

It was this article in the *Screamer* which first made Mr. Winkle aware of the condition of affairs in the room adjoining his own. He had been absent from the hotel for some hours, and had, therefore, known nothing of the sad happenings so near him. He dashed down into the office with the paper in his hand and asked for Mr. Boler; but that gentleman was not visible. It was said that he was in consultation with Dr. Ralston at the office of the latter, whereupon Mr. Winkle re-read the entire article aloud to the imperturbable clerk and expressed himself as under the impression that something was the matter with the law, or else that a certain reporter for the *Screamer* was the most dangerous lunatic at present outside of the legislature. The clerk smiled. A young man leaning against the desk made a note on a tablet, and then asked Mr. Winkle what he knew of the case and to state his objections to the law, first saying *which* law he so vigorously disapproved. The clerk winked at Mr. Winkle, but Mr. Winkle either did not see, or else did not regard the purport of the demonstration, and proceeded to express himself with a good deal of emphasis in regard to a condition of affairs which made it possible to elect as lawmakers men capable of framing such idiotic measures and employing on newspapers others who upheld the enactment. But before he had gone far in these strictures on public affairs as now administered he espied John Boler and followed him hastily upstairs.

That afternoon Mr. Winkle almost fell from his chair when he saw the evening edition of the *Screamer* with a three-column "interview" with himself. It was headed, "*Rank Socialism at the Boler House. A Close Friend of the Offending Landlord Lets the Cat out of the Bag. A Dangerous Nest of Law Breakers. John Boler and Dr. Ralston still Defiant. Backed by a Man Who Ought to Know Better. Shameless Confession of one of the Arch Conspirators. The Mask torn from Old Silas Winkle Who Roomed Next to the Would-be Suicide. Will the Police Act Now?*"

When Mr. Winkle read the article appended to these startling headlines, he descended hastily to the office floor and proceeded to make some remarks which it would be safe to assert would not be repeated by any Sunday-school superintendent—in the presence of his class—in the confines of the State of New York. John Boler was present at the time and whispered aside to Mr. Winkle that a reporter for the *Screamer* and five others from as many different papers were within hearing, whereupon Mr. Winkle became more and more excited, and talked with great volubility to each and every one of the young men as they gathered about him. "*Adds Blasphemy to His Other Crimes,*" wrote one of them as his headline, and then John Boler interfered.

"Look here, boys," said he pleasantly, but with a ring of determination in his voice, "you just let Mr. Winkle alone. This sort of thing is all new to him, and he had no more to do with that girl than if his room had been in Texas." (The reporters winked at each other and one of them wrote, *Connived at by the Proprietor.*) "I put her in the room next to his. *I* helped the doctor to resuscitate her. *I* positively refuse to give you her real name and present address, although I know both, and Mr. Winkle does not, and if the police court has any use for me it knows where to find me. Have a cigar?" Each reporter took a weed, and three of them went to the office of Dr. Ralston to complete their records as soon as possible.

"I'm sorry all this has happened to you in my house, Mr. Winkle," said John Boler, as they stood alone for a moment. "It is partly my fault, too," he added, in a sudden burst of contrition. "It" had carried his revenge further than he had intended. He knew how the old man's sudden outbreak of righteous indignation would go against him in the newspaper reports that would follow, and John Boler was kind-hearted as well as fearless.

"Good Lord, don't you worry about me, Johnnie!" said the old man, craning his neck to watch the retreating forms from the window. "But those young devils have gone over to the doctor's office and they'll bully him into telling where the girl is, and then they'll bully the police into dragging her into court yet. Dear me, dear me!"

"Now, don't you be scared about that, Mr. Winkle. The doctor and I have made up our minds to fight this thing out. We've found out all about the girl and that it was simply a case of utter despair. It was a question of death by slow or by quick means. Society, law, prescribed the slow method, and the girl herself chose the rapid one. Well, now, as long as she was to be the sufferer in either case, it strikes me that she had about as good a right to a voice in the matter as the rest of us. Dr. Ralston and I checkmated her. (I can't afford to have that kind of thing happen in the hotel, of course.) But, by gad, we're not going to let them make a criminal of her. All the circumstances combined to do that before and she chose death. Well, we stopped her efforts in that line too, and now the court proposes to put the finishing touches on society's other inhumanities and send her up for it. Why, good God, man, just look at it! In substance that girl said, 'I'll die before I'll be forced into association with criminals,' and the court says, 'You shall do nothing of the kind. Science shall doctor you up and we will *send* you up. Despair is a crime.' That girl tried every way she knew of to live right. She failed. No work that she could do came her way. Well, now, will you just tell me what she was to do? You know what any man on God's earth would do if *he* had been situated that way and *could* have sold his virtue—in the sense we use virtue for women. Well, some women are not built that way. They prefer to die. Life don't mean enough of happiness to them to pay for the rest of it—life as it is, I mean. Well, since women don't have anything to say about what the laws and social conditions shall be, it strikes me that the situation is a trifle arbitrary, to put it mildly. We make laws for and demands upon women that no man on earth would think of complying with, and then we tell 'em they sha'n't even die to get away from the conditions we impose and about which they are not allowed a word to say. To tell you the bald truth *I'm* ashamed of it. So when we learned that girl's story we just made up our minds that since we had taken the liberty to keep her from getting out of the world by a shorter cut than the one usually prescribed in such cases—starvation—that we'd just take the additional liberty of keeping her from being hounded to insanity and made a criminal of by legal verdict."

Mr. Winkle gave a snort that startled John Boler, for he had been running on half to himself during the last of his talk and had almost forgotten that the old man was present. When he heard the explosion he mistook its meaning and his conscience gave him another smart twinge.

"Yes, I'm sorry, *very* sorry, Mr. Winkle, that this trouble has come to you in my house, but who could have foreseen that—a—that is to say—"

"Trouble to *me?*" exclaimed Mr. Winkle. "Trouble to *me?* Who's said anything about any trouble to me? Do you suppose I care what those young scamps say about me in the papers? Got to make a living, haven't they? Well, society doesn't object to their making a living by taking what does not belong to 'em, if it happens to be a man's reputation or a woman's chance to ever make an honest living again. Little thefts like that don't count That is not a crime; but dear me, Johnnie, do you suppose I care a tinker's dam about that, so far as *I* go? God bless my soul, if the dear boys can sell their three columns of rot about me, and it will keep them off the heels of some poor devil that it might ruin, why, I'm satisfied. All I've got to say to you is, if they arrest you I'll go bail, and if they fine you I'll pay it, and if they jail you—hang it, Johnnie, I'll serve your term, that's all."

Mr. Boler laughed. "My punishment shall all be vicarious then, hey? Good idea, only it won't work in every-day life. The law doesn't let other people serve out your term. But I'm just as much obliged, and—and—to tell you the truth, Mr. Winkle, I'm—that is to say, I hope you will forgive me—the fact is, I forgive you freely for the part you took in helping to addle such brains as I had when I was a child. There is my hand. 'It' went a little too far this time, and—"

Mr. Winkle took off his glasses and polished them carefully. Then he placed them astride his nose and gazed thoughtfully at his old friend's son for fully a minute before he said a word. Finally he took the extended hand, shook it solemnly, and walked slowly away, wondering to himself if it could be possible that hard-headed old John Boler's son was touched a little in the brain. Mr. Boler noticed his perplexed expression and laughed merrily to himself as he started toward the elevator. Before he reached it he turned and beckoned to Mr. Winkle to follow him. On the third floor they were joined by Dr. Ralston.

"She is so much better now, Mr. Winkle," explained the genial hotel man, "and you are an older man than either the doctor or I, so I thought— It just struck me that she might feel— That you might like— Oh, damn it, would you like to go up to see her? We are going now. A clergyman has called, and if she wants to see him we shall not stay but a minute; but as there is no woman about, as she is so alone, I thought perhaps she might like to have an older man come with us, for she seems to be a very sensitive girl. She has been silent about herself so far; but she is better now, and we want to find out what work she can do, and have a place ready for her when she is able to get about. Perhaps she will talk more freely to you."

The old gentleman looked perplexed, but made no reply until they were out of the elevator. Then he took Mr. Boler by the arm and said helplessly, "I— I am a bachelor, you know, Johnnie, and—"

"No!" laughed Mr. Boler. "Well, confound it, you don't look it. Anybody would take you for the proud father of a large brood. She will think you are and it may help her. Come on."

The old gentleman entered the darkened room last and sat down silently in the deepest shadow. The doctor stepped to the bed and spoke in a low tone. A white face on the pillow turned slowly, so that the only band of light that reached in from the open door fell full upon it. Mr. Winkle shuddered as he saw for the first time the delicate, pallid, hopeless face.

"A priest?" she said feebly, in answer to the doctor. "Oh, no. Why should I want to see a priest? You've had your way. You've brought me back to battle with a world wherein I only now acknowledged my defeat." Her voice trembled with weakness and emotion, but she was looking steadily at the doctor with great wide eyes, in which there burnt the intensity of mental suffering and a determination to free her mind even at the risk of losing the good-will of those who had intended to be kind to her. "A priest! What could he do? *This* life is what I fear. His mission is to deal with other worlds—of which I know already what he does—and that is *nothing*. Of this life I know, alas! too much. Far more than he. He cannot help me, for I could tell him much he *cannot* know, of suffering and fortitude and hope laid low at last, without a refuge even in cloistered walls. I know what he would say. His voice would tremble and he would offer sympathy and good advice—and, maybe, alms. These are not what I want or need. I am not very old—just twenty-two—but I have thought and thought until my brain is tired, and what good could it do for him to sit beside me here and say in gentle tones that it is very sad? No doubt that he would tell me, too, how wicked I have been that I should choose to die by my own hand when life had failed me."

She smiled a little, and her wan face lit from within was beautiful still in spite of its pallor. The doctor murmured something about natural sympathy, and Mr. Boler remarked that men who were fortunate would gladly help those who were in distress if only they knew in time. She did not appear to heed them, but presently went on as though her mind were on the clergymen below waiting to see her.

"To feel that it is sad is only human; but what is to be done? That is the question now. What is to be done for suffering in *this* world? It is life that is hard to bear, not death. Sympathy with the unfortunate is good. Kind words and gentle tones as your priest recounts their woes are touching. Yes, and when they are drawn to fit the truth would melt a heart of stone; but unless action wings the sympathy and dries the tears, the object of his tenderness is in no wise bettered—indeed, is injured. Why? Because he lulls to sleep man's conscience and thereby gives relief from pangs that otherwise had found an outlet through an open purse. And when I say an open purse I do not speak of charity, that double blight which kills the self-respect in its recipient and numbs the conscience of the 'benevolent' man who grasps the utmost penny *here* that he may give with ostentation *there*, wounding the many that he may heal the few. All this was safe enough, no doubt, while Poverty was ignorant, for ignorance is helpless always; but now—" There was a pause. She raised her head a little from the pillow and a frightened look crept into her eyes— "but now the poor are not so ignorant that it will long be safe to play at cross purposes with suffering made too intelligent to drink in patient faith the bitter draughts of life and wait the crown of gold he promises hereafter—and wears, meanwhile, himself. A *little* joy on earth, they think, will not bedim the lustre of a life that is to come—if such there be. You see I've thought a little in these wretched days and months just past." She was silent again for a moment. A bitter smile crossed her face and vanished. The doctor offered her a powder which she swallowed without a word. John Boler stepped to the table and poured out a glass of wine, but when he held it toward her she shook her head and closed her eyes a moment. Then she spoke again as if no break had checked her thought. "Oh, no; I do not care to see your priest. The poor no longer fail to note his willingness to risk the needle's eye with camel's back piled high with worldly gain. If he may enter thus, why may not they with simpler train and fewer trappings? The poor are asking this to-day of prince and priest alike. No answer comes from either. Evasion does not satisfy. I ask, but no one answers. The day once was when silence passed for wisdom. That day is gone. To-day we are asking why? and why? and why? no longer, when? And so the old reply, 'hereafter,' does not fit the query. Why, not when, is what we urge to-day, and your replies must change to fit the newer, nearer question. When I say *your* replies, I do not mean you, doctor, nor your friend. You two meant kindly by me. Yes, I know. I am not claiming that you are at fault, nor they—the fortunate—the prince and priest. I understand. Blind nature took her course and trod beneath her cruel feet the millions who were born too weak to struggle with the foes they found within themselves and in their stronger brothers. I know, I know."

She lay back on the pillow and closed her eyes wearily. Mr. Winkle drew near and stood behind the doctor's chair, still keeping in the shadow, but watching her pale face with an intensity born of a simple nature easy to stir and quick to resolve. The doctor touched her pulse with a light finger and gravely nodded his head as he glanced at his watch. Her heavy eyelids did not lift but her voice broke the silence again. There was a cadence in it that gave a solemn thrill to the three men as they listened, the doctor watching with professional interest the effect of the powder he had given; the other two waited, expecting they knew not what.

"The ignorance and cruelty of all the past, the superstitious fears, the cunning prophecies, the greeds and needs of men, joined hands and marched triumphant. They did not halt to ask the fallen what had borne them down. They did not silence bugle blasts of joy where new-made graves were thick. No silken flag was lowered to warm to life the shivering forms of comrades overcome and fallen by the way. The strong marched on and called themselves the brave. Sometimes they were. But other times the bravest had gone down, plucked at, perchance, by wife or child or friend whose sorrow or distress reached out and twined itself about the strong but tender heart and held it back until the foot lost step, and in the end the eye lost sight of those who only now had kept him company."

She lifted her small white hand and pointed as if to a distant battlefield, but her eyes remained closed. The doctor glanced uneasily at his watch and took her other wrist in his fingers again.

"The next battalion trampled him. The priest bent low and whispered 'over there, hereafter,' and slipped the treasure of the fallen hero beneath his ample robe to swell the coffers of the church, since dead men need no treasures."

Her voice was infinitely sad but she laughed a little and opened her eyes. They fixed themselves upon the silvered head of Mr. Winkle standing behind the doctor's chair.

"Perhaps I shock you. I do not mean to, but I have thought and thought these last few wretched months, and looking at the battlefields of life backward through all the ages, I thought I saw at night, in camp, the priest and conqueror meet beside the campfire and council for the next day's march. I thought I heard the monarch say, 'I go before and cleave my way. You follow me and gather up two things—the spoils I miss and all the arrows of awakened scorn and wrath embedded in the breasts of those of our own ranks who fall or are borne down, lest they arise and overtake us while we sleep and venge themselves on us. Tell them to wait. Their time will come. Tell them *I* clear the way for them, and *you* forgive a hatred which you see is growing up within their wicked breasts. Quiet, soothe, and shame them into peace. Assure them that *hereafter* they, not we, shall have the better part. Gain time. Lay blame to me if need be; but always counsel patience, waiting, acquiescence, peace, submission to the will of God—*your will and mine.* Your task is easy. No danger lies therein. I take the risk and share with you the glory and the gain.' I heard the priest disclaim all greed of gain and go to do his part as loyal subject and as holy man. I saw all this and more before I took the last resolve you balked. You meant it kindly, doctor, yes, I know, but I am very tired and what is there ahead for me, or such as I, on battlefields like these?"

No one ventured a reply. She closed her eyes and waited. The doctor took another powder from his case and held it above her lips. She smiled and swallowed it.

"We take our powders very docilely," she said, with a bitter little laugh as the wine-glass left her hand and Mr. Boler's finger touched her own. He noticed that hers was very cold.

"They used to make us sleep in the good old days of priest and monarch, but our nerves are wrong just now. Our powders only make us think the more and have strange visions."

Dr. Ralston glanced at Mr. Boler and nodded his head mysteriously. The powder was beginning to work, he thought, for she had reverted to the old vision, and talked as if she were in a dream. "That way it was, another way it is, and still another will be," she was saying. "To-day the honest poor, the hampered weak, are defeated, dazed, and some of us are hopeless. Others there are who cling to hope and life and brood on vengeance. That is your danger, gentlemen, for days that are to come. You will have to change your powders. The old prescriptions do not make us sleep. We think, and think, and think. We strain our nerves and break our hearts, for what? A life as cold and colorless and sad as death itself—to some of us far sadder—and yet you will not even let us die. Again we ask you, why? There is no place on earth for such as we, unless we will be criminals. That is the hinge whereon the future turns. How many will prefer the crime to want? What dangers lie behind the door that now is swinging open? Intelligence has taught us scorn for such a grovelling lot, has multiplied our needs, and turned the knife of suffering in quivering wounds no longer deadened by the anaesthetics of ignorant content with life or superstitious fear of death. The door is swinging on the hinge. The future has to face creatures the past has made like demons. Some, like myself, behind the door, who do not love mere life, will turn the sharpened dagger on themselves. But there are others—"

Her voice sank. The three men thought that she had fallen asleep at last. The doctor drew a long satisfied breath and consulted his watch for the fourth time, making a mental note for future use in giving the drug whose action he was watching. He started and frowned, therefore, when her voice broke the silence again.

"Others there are, in spite of pain and anguish, in spite of woe and fear, who cling to life—who read in eyes they worship the pangs of hunger, cold, and mental agony. Where will their vengeance go? Who knows?"

She opened her great eyes and looked first at one and then at another, and repeated, "Who knows?"

Again there was no reply. After a long pause Mr. Winkle said gently:

"There is a place in life for girls like you. I shall charge myself with it. You shall find work and joy yet, my child. Now go to sleep. Be quiet. We have let you talk too long. Stop thinking sadly now. You think too much. You *think* too much."

She closed her eyes quickly and there was a tightening of the lips that left them paler than before. Then a tear rolled slowly down her temple. Before it reached the pillow the doctor bent forward and dried it softly with his silk handkerchief. She opened her eyes wide at the touch. "'Be quiet?'" she repeated, "'stop thinking?' Oh, yes; *I* will be quiet, but the rest, the others? Those with whom you do not charge yourself, who find no work, no joy? Will *they* be quiet, will they stop thinking? Oh, yes; I can be quiet, very quiet, but the rest, the rest? The others who think too much—*all, all?*"

There was a wild look in her dry eyes. The doctor touched her wrist again and said softly to the men beside him, "It is working now. She will sleep. But the shock of all her trouble has left her mind unhinged, poor child. 'The rest? the others?' *We* cannot care for all the countless poor. Her brain is surely touched, poor child, poor child. How can we tell whether the others will stop thinking, or how, or when? Her mind was wandering, and now she sleeps, poor child. Come out. She is best alone."

They closed the door gently behind them and stood a moment in awkward silence outside, each one afraid to speak and yet ashamed of his own tender helplessness. At last Mr. Winkle looking steadily in the crown of his hat, said huskily, "By gad, boys, there is something rotten in the state of Denmark." They all three laughed with an effort, but kept their eyes averted.

"It is a rat in the wainscoting of the storeroom," said John Boler, with a desperate attempt to regain his old manner and tone, "and I've got to go and look after it or there'll be the devil to pay with the Boler House." And he ran down the stairs three steps at a time heartily ashamed of his own remark, but determined not to allow the tears to show themselves either in his eyes or voice, and feeling that his only safety was in flight.

But Mr. Winkle had not stood silently behind the doctor's chair all that time for nothing, and if his nature was somewhat light, and if he had taken life so far as something of a jest, he was by no means without a heart. He did not now trouble himself very greatly about the tangled problems of existence, but he felt quite equal to dealing with any given case effectively and on short notice. With systems he was helpless, with individuals he could deal promptly. Therefore he, in common with the doctor and Mr. Boler, and, indeed, with most of us, occupied himself with the girl he saw suffering and in need.

When she had cried out, "But the rest, the others, what of them?" he had said nothing, because he had nothing to say. He was vaguely aware that when the smallpox broke out on one of Dr. Ralston's patients that astute practitioner did not essay to treat each individual pustule separately as the whole of the disease and so devote his entire skill and mind to each in turn until it was cured. But then he could not undertake to cure the whole human race of its various social ailments any more than Dr. Ralston could hope to look after all of its physical pains. So Mr. Winkle took this one little social pustule upstairs as his particular charge, and in his own peculiar way went about securing better conditions for her, leaving the "others who think too much" to somebody else, or to fate, as the case might be. Therefore, when Mr. Winkle reached the street door and met an officer of the law who had come prepared to learn the whereabouts of the would-be suicide or else take Mr. John Boler and Dr. Ralston into custody, the old gentleman made up his mind to begin his part in the future proceedings without further delay.

Unknown to Mr. Winkle himself, literature had lost a great novelist when he had gone into the mercantile business, and the surprises which he now sprang upon the policeman were no less astonishing and interesting to himself than they were to that astute guardian of the public morals.

"Want to know where she is, do you? Well, don't worry Johnnie Boler any more. They've already got him so his mind is a little affected. I'll tell you all about that girl. Her name is Estelle Morris. She worked for me for nine years as a nursery governess. Last month my youngest child died, and it upset Estelle so that she has been out of her head ever since. I thought if I'd bring her to the city maybe she might get over it, but she didn't, and the doctor gave her some stuff and she took a double dose by mistake, and all the row came from that and the long tongues of the servants, pieced out by the long pencils of the reporters. See!"

"Is that so?" exclaimed the officer. "Where is she now?"

Mr. Winkle had not thought of that, and he did not know exactly what to say; but he agreed to produce her in court on the following day if so ordered, and there the matter dropped for the moment.

That evening there appeared in a paper this "want:" "A good-looking young woman who is willing to lie like a pirate for the space of one hour for the sum of $50. May have to go to court." The number of handsome girls who were anxious to lend the activity of their tongues for the purpose named and the amount stipulated was quite wonderful. One particularly bright young miss remarked that she had been in training for just that position for years. She was confidential correspondent for a broker. Mr. Winkle accepted her on the spot.

"Now," said he, "look solemn and sad. That is right. You do it first rate. Whatever I tell about you you are to stick to. Understand that?"

"Perfectly. Years of practice," she responded, with entire simplicity and without a suspicion of humor.

"Your name is Estelle Morris, and you have been the governess of my children for nine years. How old are you?"

"Nineteen," said Estelle Morris demurely.

"Good gracious, girl, what could you teach at ten years of age? You've got to be older. Take the curl out of your hair in front and put on a bonnet with strings. I heard my niece say that made her look ten years older. Mind you, you are not a day under twenty-six. Not a day."

"All right," said Estelle Morris thoughtfully.

"You are to look sick, too, and—"

"Oh, I can fix *that* easy enough. I'll—"

"Well, then fix it and come back here at exactly two o'clock this afternoon."

At the appointed hour, Mr. Winkle met Miss Estelle Morris and took her with great dignity and care to the Boler House, where he was joined by another gentleman—an officer of the law—and the three started out together.

"The examination was strictly private in deference to the wishes of the parties first implicated, John Boler and Dr. Ralston, and because it is now believed that the girl is more sinned against than sinning," wrote the reporter for the morning rival of the *Screamer*. "It is the object of justice to help the erring to start anew in life wherever that line of action is consonant with the stern necessities of the blind goddess. Neither of the male accomplices appeared in the case, but Mr. Silas Winkle—whose name has figured somewhat conspicuously in the matter—produced the principal, who, it must be confessed, is pretty enough to account for all the chivalry which has been displayed in her behalf. She confessed to twenty-six years of single wretchedness, although she could easily pass for a year or two younger. It would appear that she had lived in Mr. Winkle's family for nine years as governess to his children and came to the city with him about two weeks ago. The justice accepted this explanation of the relations existing between them, and that there was no attempt at suicide at all, but only an accidental overdose of a remedy prescribed by Dr. Ralston, which explained satisfactorily the doctor's connection with the unsavory case, and places him once more in the honorable position from which this unfortunate affair so nearly hurled him. In short, the justice said in substance, 'not guilty, and don't do it any more.' The young woman bowed modestly, and Silas Winkle led her from the court-room a sadder, and, let us hope, a wiser woman. Such as she must have much to live for. Many a man has braved death for a face less lovely than hers. This ends the 'Boler House Mystery,' which, after all, turns out to be only a tempest in a teapot, with a respectable father of a family and his children's governess for *dramatis persono* and a fresh young reporter on a certain sensational morning contemporary as general misinformer of the public as usual." This was headlined, "*Exploded—Another Fake by Our Esteemed Contemporary.*"

That night John Boler rubbed his eyes when he read the report. "I thought you were a bachelor, Mr. Winkle," said he, "and here you produce in court a governess—"

"I am," said Mr. Winkle, laughing, and then he showed his "want" advertisement. "That is the whole case, Johnnie, my boy, but it is all over now. Don't you worry; it might go to your head again. You saved the girl and I saved you, and it only cost me $50. I'd pay that any time to get ahead of the *Screamer*, and I rather think I salted that enterprising sheet down this time, don't you? But what is to become of that girl?" added he, without waiting for a reply to his first question. "You've taken the liberty to save her life, which she had decided she did not want under existing circumstances. Has she simply got to go over the same thing again? I told her that I'd look after her, but I don't see how in thunder I'm going to do it. She won't take money from me and *I've* got nothing for her to do. Is there nothing ahead of her but a coffin or a police court?"

"For this individual girl, yes. Dr. Ralston has already secured work for her; but for all the thou-sands of her kind—" John Boler's voice trembled a little and he stopped speaking to hide it. He in common with most men was heartily ashamed of his better nature.

"For all the thousands of her kind," broke in Mr. Winkle, "there are just exactly three roads open—starvation, suicide, or shame, with the courts, the legislature, and the newspapers on the side of the latter. I just tell you, Johnnie, it makes my blood boil. I—I don't see any way out of it—none at all. That is the worst of it."

"I do," said Mr. Boler.

"*You do!*" exclaimed Mr. Winkle excitedly, and then looked hard at his old friend's son to see if he had gone crazy again.

"Yes, I do. Those same newspapers you are so down on will do it. They're bound to. The boys go wrong sometimes, as they did in this case; but that only makes sensible people indignant, and, after all, it called attention to the law that makes such things possible. *More light on the laws.* That's the first thing we want, and no matter which side of a question the papers take, we are bound to get that in the long run. Silence is the worst danger. We get pretty mad at the boys if they write what we don't like, but that isn't half so dangerous as if they didn't write at all. See?"

Mr. Winkle turned slowly away and shook his head as he murmured to himself: "Who would have believed that old John Boler would have been the father of a lunatic? Dear me, dear me. I'm going back to Meadville before I get touched in the head myself." And he started to his room to pack his valise. John Boler followed him to the elevator.

"I don't blame you for feeling pretty mad about all the stuff they put in the *Screamer* about you; but—oh, the boys *mean* all right—"

"So does the devil," broke in the old man. But Mr. Boler gave no evidence of noticing the interruption nor of observing the irascibility of his guest.

"The trouble is with the system," he went on, entering the elevator after Mr. Winkle. "Why, just look at it, man. What I say or do, if it is of a public nature, I'm responsible for *to* the public. What you write you put your name to; but it's a pretty big temptation to a young fellow who knows he has got the swing in a newspaper and doesn't have to sign his name to what he says, to make an effort to 'scoop' his rivals at whatever cost. The boys don't mean any harm, but irresponsible power is a mighty dangerous weapon to handle. Not many older men can be trusted to use it wisely. Then why should we expect it of those young fellows who don't know yet any of the deeper meanings of life? Great Scott, man! *I* think they do pretty well under the circumstances. I'm afraid I'd do worse."

Mr. Winkle stroked his chin reflectively.

"No doubt, no doubt," he said abstractedly, as they stepped out of the elevator.

John Boler looked at him for a brief space of time to see if he had intended the thrust and then went on:

"That girl's life or death just meant an item to the boys, and it didn't mean much more to you or me until—until we stood and heard her talk and saw her suffer, and were made personally uncomfortable by it. Yet we are old enough to know all about it for her and others. We *do* know it, and go right along as if we didn't. We are a pretty bad lot, don't you think so?"

Silas Winkle unlocked his door before he spoke. Then he turned to his old friend's son and shook his hand warmly.

"Good-bye," he said, looking at him steadily. "Good-bye, Johnnie. I see it only comes on you at odd spells. Come up to Meadville for a while and I think you will get over it altogether. Your father was the clearest-headed man I ever saw and you seem to have lucid intervals. Those last remarks of yours were worthy of your father, my boy," and the old man patted him softly on the back.

John Boler whistled all the way downstairs. Then he laughed.

"I wonder if old Winkle really does think I am off my base," said he, as he took down his hat. "I suppose we are all more or less crazy. He thinks I am and I know he is. It is a crazy world. Only lunatics could plan or conduct it on its present lines." And he laughed again and then sighed and passed out into the human stream on Broadway.

THE TIME LOCK OF OUR ANCESTORS.

"Visiting the iniquity of the fathers upon the children unto the third and fourth generation."—Bible.

"Don't be so hard on yourself, Nellie. I am sure it can be no great wrong you have done. Girls like you are too apt to be morbid. No doubt we all do it, whatever it is. I'm sure I shall not blame you when you tell me. Perhaps I shall say you are quite right—that is, if there is any right and wrong to it, and provided I know which is which, after I hear the whole story—as most likely I shall not. Right—"

And here the elder woman smiled a little satirically, and looked out of the window with a far-away gaze, as if she were retravelling through vast spaces of time and experience far beyond anything her friend could comprehend.

The evening shadows had gathered, and cast, as they will, a spell of gravity and exchange of confidences over the two.

Presently the older woman began speaking again:

"Do you know, Nell, I was always a little surprised that Lord Byron, of all people, should have put it that way:

"I know the right, and I approve it too;

Condemn the wrong—and yet the wrong pursue.

"*The* right '—why, it is like a woman to say that. As if there were but one 'right,' and it were dressed in purple and fine linen, and seated on a throne in sight of the assembled multitude! '*The right.*' indeed! Yes, it sounds like a woman—and a very young woman at that, Nellie."

The girl looked with large, troubled, passionate eyes at her friend, and then broke out into hot, indignant words—words that would have offended many a woman; but Florence Campbell only laughed, a light, queer little peal; tipped her chair a trifle farther back, put her daintily slippered feet on the satin cushion of the low window-seat, and looked at her friend, through the gathering darkness, from under half-closed eyelids.

Presently—this woman was always deliberate in her conversation; long silences were a part of her power in interesting and keeping the full attention of her listeners—presently she said:

"Of course you think so. Why shouldn't you? So did I—once. And do you know, Nellie, that sort of sentiment dies hard—*very* hard—in a woman. At your age—" Florence Campbell always spoke as if she were very old, although to look at her one would say that she was not twenty-eight.

These delicately formed Dresden-china women often carry their age with such an easy grace—it sits upon them so lightly—in spite of ill-health, mental storms, and moral defeats, that while their more robust sisters grow haggard and worn, and hard of feature and tone, under weights less terrible and with feelings less intense, they keep their grace and gentleness of tone in the teeth of every blast.

"At your age, dear, I would have scorned a woman who talked as I do now; and more than that, I would have suspected her, as you do not suspect me, of being a very dangerous and not unlikely a very bad person indeed—simply from choice. While you—you generous little soul—think that I am better than I talk."

She laughed again, and shifted her position as if she were not wholly comfortable under the troubled gaze of the great eyes she knew were fastened upon her.

"You think I am better than my opinions. I know exactly what you tell yourself about me when you are having it out with yourself upstairs. Oh, I know! You excuse me for saying this on the theory that it was not deliberate—was an oversight. You account for that by the belief that I am not well—my nerves are shaken. You are perfectly certain that *I* am all right, no matter what I do, or say, or think." She took her little friend's soft hand as it twisted nervously a ribbon in her lap, and held the back of it against her cheek, as she often did. "But just suppose it were some one else—some other woman, Nellie, you would suspect her (no doubt quite unfairly) of all the crimes in the statute-books. Oh, I know, I know, child! I did—at your age—and, sad to relate, *I* had no Florence Campbell to soften my judgments on even one of my sex."

She had grown serious as she talked, and her voice almost trembled. The instant she recognized this herself, she laughed again, and said gayly:

"Oh, I was a very severe judge—once—I do assure you, though you may not think so now." She dropped her voice to a tone of mocking solemnity, not uncommon with her, and added: "If you won't tell on me, I'll make a little confession to you, dear;" and she took both of the girl's hands firmly in her own and waited until the promise was given.

"I wouldn't have it get out for the world, but the fact is, Nell, I sometimes strongly suspect that, at your age, I was—a most unmitigated, self-righteous little prig."

Nellie's hands gave a disappointed little jerk: but her friend held them firmly, laughed gayly at her discomfiture—for she recognized fully that the girl was attuned to tragedy—buried her face in them! for an instant, and then deliberately kissed in turn each pink little palm—not omitting her own. Then she dropped those of her friend, and leaned back against her cushions and sighed.

Nellie was puzzled and annoyed. She was on the verge of tears.

"Florence, darling," she said presently, "if I did not know you to be the best woman in the world, I shouldn't know what to make of your dark hints, and of—and of you. You are always a riddle to me—a beautiful riddle, with a good answer, if only I could guess it. You talk like a fiend, sometimes, and you act like—an angel, always."

"Give me up. You can't guess me. Fact is, I haven't got any answer," laughed Florence.

But the girl went steadily on without seeming to hear her: "Do you know, there are times when I wonder if it would be possible to be insane and vicious, mentally and *verbally*, as it were, and perfectly sane and exaltedly good morally."

Florence Campbell threw herself back on her cushions and laughed gayly, albeit a trifle hysterically. "Photograph taken by an experienced artist!" she exclaimed. "You've hit me! Oh, you've hit me, Nell." Then sitting suddenly bolt-upright, she looked the girl searchingly in the face, and said slowly: "Do you know, Nellie, that I am sometimes tempted to tell the truth? About myself, I mean—and to *you*. Never on any other subject, nor to anybody else, of course," she added dryly, in comedy tones, strangely contrasting with the almost tragic accents as she went on. "But I can't. '*The* truth!' Why, it is like *the* right; I'm sure I don't know what it is; and it has been so long—oh, so cruelly long—since I told it, by word or action, that I have lost its very likeness from my mind. I have told lies and acted lies so long—" Her friend's eyes grew indignant and she began to protest, but Florence ran on: "I have evaded facts—not only to others, but to myself, until—until I'd have to swear out a search-warrant and have it served on my mental belongings to find out myself what I *do* think or feel or want on any given subject."

It was characteristic of the woman to use this flippant method of expression, even in her most intense moments.

"I change so, Nell; sometimes suddenly—all in a flash."

There was a long silence. Then she began again, quite seriously:

"There is a theory, you know, that we inherit traits and conditions from our remote ancestors as well as from our immediate ones. I sometimes fancy that they descend to some people with a Time Lock attachment. A child is born"—she held out her hands as if a baby lay on them—"he is like his mother, we will say, gentle, sweet, kind, truthful, for years—let us say seven. Suddenly the Time Lock turns, and the traits of his father (modified, of course, by the acquired habits of seven years) show themselves strongly— take possession, in fact. Another seven years, and the priggishness of a great-uncle, the stinginess of an aunt, or the dullness, in books, of a rural grandfather. Then, in keeping with the next two turns of the Lock, he falls in love with every new face he sees, marries early and indulges himself recklessly in a large family. He is an exemplary husband and father, as men go, an ideal business man, and a general favorite in society."

She was running on now as if her words had the whip-hand of her.

"Everybody remarks upon the favorable change since his stupid, priggish college days. All this time, through every change, he has been honorable and upright in his dealings with his fellows. Suddenly the Time Lock of a Thievish Ancestor is turned on; he finds temptation too strong for even that greatly under-estimated power—the force of habit of a lifetime—and the trust funds in his keeping disappear with him to Canada. Everybody is surprised, shocked, pained—and he, no doubt, more so than any one else. Emotional insanity is offered as a possible explanation by the charitable; longheaded, calculating, intentional rascality, by the severe or self-righteous. And he? Well, he is wholly unable to account for it at all. He *knows* that he had not lived all these years as a conscious, self-controlled thief. He *knows* that the temptations of his past life had never before taken that particular form. He *knows* that the impulse was sudden, blinding, overwhelming; but he does not know why and how. It was like an awful dream. He seemed to be powerless to overcome it. The Time Lock had turned without his knowledge, and in spite of himself. The unknown, unheard-of Thievish Ancestor took possession, as it were, through force of superior strength and ability—and then it was his hour. The hereditary shadow on the dial had come around to him. The great-uncle's hour was past. *He*, no doubt, was 'turned on' to some other dazed automaton—in Maine or Texas—who had fallen heir to a drop too much of his blood, and she, poor thing, if it happened to be a girl this time, forthwith proceeded to fall in love with her friend's husband—seeing he was the only man at hand at the time; while the Thievish Ancestor left— in shame and contrition—a small but light-fingered boy in Georgia, to keep his engagement with our respectable, highly honored, and heretofore highly honorable man of affairs in Wall street. The Time Lock of heredity had been set for this hour, and the machinery of circumstances oiled the wheels and silently moved the dial." There was absolute silence when Florence Campbell's voice ceased. The heavy curtains made the shadows in the struggling moonlight deep and solemn. Two great eyes looked out into the darkness and a shudder passed over her frame. She thought her little friend had fallen asleep, she lay so still and quiet on the rug at her feet. Florence sighed, and thought how quickly youth forgot its troubles and how lightly Care sat on her throne. Then suddenly a passionate sobbing broke the silence, and two arms, covered with lace and jewels, flung themselves around the older woman's knees.

"O my God! Florence; O my God! is there no way to stop the wheels? Must they go blindly on? Can we *never* know who or what we shall be to-morrow? It is awful, Florence, awful; and—it—is *true!* O God! it is *true!*"

Florence Campbell had been very serious when she stopped her little harangue. There had been a quality in her voice which, while it was not wholly new to her friend, *would* have been unknown to many who thought they knew her well. To them she was a beautiful, fashionable, rather light woman, with a gay nature, who either did not know, or did not care to investigate too closely, the career of her husband, to whom she was devotedly attached.

She had been quite serious, I say, when she stopped her little philosophical speculation; but she was greatly surprised at the storm she had raised in the breast of her little friend.

Florence bent down quickly, and putting her arms about the girl tried to raise her up; but she only sobbed the harder, and clung to her friend's knees as a desperate, frightened creature might cling to its only refuge.

"Why, Nellie, little kitten," said the older woman, using a term of endearment common with her in talking with the girl—"why, Nellie, little kitten, what in the world is the matter? Did I scare the life out of you with my Time Locks and my gruesome ancestors?" and she tried to laugh a little; but the sound of her voice was not altogether pleasant to the ear. "I'll ring for a light. I had no business to talk such stuff to you when you were blue and in the dark too. I guess, Nell, that the Time Lock of *my* remote ancestor, who was a fool, must have been turned on me shortly after sundown to-day, don't you think?" And this time her laugh lacked the note of bitterness it had held before.

She ran on, still caressing the weeping girl at her feet:

"Yes, undoubtedly, my Remote Ancestor—the fool—has now moved in. Do you think you can stand seven years of him, kitten, if you live with me that long? But you won't. You'll go and marry some horrid man, and I shall be so jealous that my hair will curl at sight of him."

But the girl would not laugh. She refused to be cheered, nor would she have a light. She raised herself until her head rested on her friend's bosom, and clung to her, sobbing as if her heart would break. Florence stroked her hair and sat silent for a while, wondering just what had so shaken the child. She knew full well that it was *not* what she had hinted of the darkness and her gruesome story. Presently Nellie drew her friend's face down, and whispered between her sobs:

"Darling, I must have had some dreadful ancestor, a wicked—*wicked* woman. I—"

Florence Campbell shrieked with laughter. She felt relieved of—she did not know what. She had blamed herself for even unconsciously touching the secret spring of sorrow in the girl's heart. It was a strange sight, the two women clinging to each other, the one sobbing, the other laughing, each trying in vain to check the other.

At last Nellie said, still almost in a whisper: "But, Florence, you do not know. You do not understand. You are too good to know. It is you who will scorn and hate me when I tell you. O Florence, Florence, I can never *dare* to tell you!" Her friend, still laughing, made little ejaculations of satirical import as the girl grew more and more hysterical.

"O thou wicked wretch!" laughed she. "No doubt you've killed your man, as they say out West. Oh, dear—oh, dear! Nell, this is really quite delicious! Did it step on a bug? Or was it a great big spider? And does it think it ought to be hanged for the crime? A peal of laughter from the one, a shudder from the other, was the only reply to these efforts to break the force of the girl's self-reproach. Florence clinched her small fist in mock heroics and began again:

"Your crimes have found you out! And mine—*mine*—has been the avenging hand! Really, this is too good, kitten. I shall tell, let me see—I shall tell—*Tom!*"

The girl was on her feet in a flash.

"Not that! *not that*, Florence! Anything but that! I will tell you myself first—*he* shall not?" Florence grew suddenly silent and grave. The girl slipped down at her knees again, and clasping her hand, went hoarsely on:

"O Florence, darling, I did not mean to wrong you! Truly, truly, I did not—and I do not believe *he* did—not at—first. We—oh, it was—" she sank on the floor, at the feet of her astonished friend, and with upstretched arms in the darkness whispered: "Florence, Florence—O my God! I *cannot* tell you! I must go away! *I must go away!*" The older woman did not touch the outstretched hands and they sank to the floor, and on them rested a tear-stained, wretched face.

A moment later Tom Campbell entered the room. To eyes unaccustomed to the darkness nothing was visible. He did not see his wife, who arose as he entered, and stood with bated breath over the form of the girl on the floor.

"By Jove!" he muttered, "this room is as dark as Egypt, and then some—Wonder where Florence is. Those damned servants ought to be shot! Whole house like a confounded coal-pit! Didn't expect me for hours yet, I suppose! That's no reason for living like a lot of damned bats! 'Fraid of mosquitoes, I suppose. Where are those matches? *Florence!* She's evidently gone out—or to bed. Wonder where her little 'kitten' is? Umm—wonder how much longer Florence means to keep her here? Don't see how the thing's going to go on much longer this way, with a girl with a conscience like that. Perfectly abnormal! Perfectly ridiculous! Umm—no more tact than—"

Nellie moaned aloud. Florence had held her breath, hoping he would go. He had almost reached the door leading to the hall, after his vain search for matches.

"Hello! what was that?" said Campbell, turning again into the room.

His wife knew that escape was not now possible. "Nothing, Tom," she said, in a voice that trembled a little. "Go upstairs. I will come up soon."

"Why, hello, Florence, that you? What are you sitting here in the dark for, all alone? Why didn't you speak to me when I came in? What did you let me—"

Nellie sat up, and in doing so overturned a chair.

Tom's eyes had grown accustomed to the darkness. He saw the two women outlined before him, and he saw that Nellie had been on the floor, and that his wife stood over her.

"What's the matter?" he demanded. "What's up?"

He came toward them. Nellie sprang to her feet, with flashing eyes and outstretched, imploring hands to wave him back. She was about to rush into a painful explanation. Florence stepped toward her, put both arms about her, and drew her onto the cushioned window-seat at their side. She knew she must cover the girl's agitation from her husband, and somehow gain time to think.

"Sit down, dear," she said softly. "Sit down here by me. You have been asleep. He frightened you coming in so suddenly. You have been dreaming; you talked in your sleep—but it was all nonsense—about an ancestor, whom you blamed very bitterly."

The girl began to speak impulsively, but Florence checked her.

"Yes, I know. You told me. It was all the greatest stuff. But the part that was true—I doubt if she was to blame. I think, from all I know of—of her, and of the gentleman you mentioned, the one she—seemed to care for—that—oh, no, kitten! I am *sure she* was not to blame."

Nellie was trembling violently, clinging to her friend in shame and remorse. Tom stood perfectly quiet in the deeper darkness, back from the window, with a smile on his cheerful face and a puzzled light in his handsome eyes.

"Go upstairs, Tom," said Florence again, this time in a steadier tone. "Nellie's head aches; you waked her up too suddenly. We don't want more light—do we, Nellie? Not just now. We have quite light enough for the present. I assure you we are better off just now in the dark. You would think so yourself if you could see us as we see ourselves. We are quite battered and out at elbow, I assure you, and not at all fit for fastidious masculine eyes."

She was pulling herself up well. "To-morrow we will spruce up our bangs, put on fresh gowns, and not know ourselves for the wretches we are tonight. Until then, Sir Knight, no masculine eye shall rest upon our dilapidation. Go!"

Tom Campbell had seen his wife in this mood before. He went.

All the way upstairs he wondered what had happened. "Never could make women out anyway," he muttered; "least of all, Florence. Women are a queer lot. More you live with 'em, more you don't know what they'll do next. Wonder what in thunder's up. 'Kitten' never said a word; but I'm damned if I did't hear her groan! Guess the little goose feels kind of—queer—with me and the old lady both present. Wonder—whew!—wonder how much I said aloud, and how much they heard when I first went in! Confounded habit, talking aloud to myself! Got to stop it, old boy; must be done—get you into trouble yet!"

Then he turned off the gas, and was sleeping as peacefully as an infant before the two women below stairs had parted for the night.

When Tom left the room, Nellie began to sob again, and Florence stroked her hair with her icy hands and waited for the girl to speak—or grow calm. And for herself—she hardly knew what she waited for in herself; but she felt that she needed time.

After a long silence she said, quite gently; "Nellie, little girl, we will go upstairs now; you will go to bed. If you ever feel like it, after you take time to think it over, and your nerves are quiet—if you ever feel like it, you may tell just what trick your troublesome ancestor has tried to play you; but I want to say now, dear, don't feel that you *must* tell me, nor that I do not know perfectly well that my little kitten is all right, ancestors or no ancestors, and that we, together can somehow find the combination to that Time Lock that so distresses you, and turn it off again. Meantime, little girl *no one* shall harm you. You shall be let alone; you are all right! Be *sure* of that. I am. Now, good-night;" and she kissed the still sobbing girl on the forehead and hands, in spite, of her protests and self-accusations.

Suddenly Nellie sank on her knees again, and grasped Florence's dress as she had turned to go:

"O Florence! O Florence! are you human? How *can* you? You are not like other women! O my God! if I could only be like you; but you frighten me! You are so calm. How cold your hands are! oh—"

"Are they? I did not notice. Oh well, no matter; it is an old trick of theirs, you know."

Florence Campbell's voice was very steady now. Her words were slow and deliberate—they sounded as if she was very tired; and her step, as she climbed the stairs, had lost its spring and lightness.

The next morning Nellie's breakfast was carried to her room, with a message from Florence not to get up until she came to her at their usual hour for reading together.

About noon, as the girl lay thinking for the hundredth time that she must get up and face life again—that she must somehow stop this blinding headache, and go away—that she must die—Florence swept into the room, trailing her soft, long gown behind her, and gently closed the door. She had put on a gay pink tea-gown, with masses of white lace and smart little bows in unexpected places.

"Feel better, dear?" she asked, gayly. "Griggs told me your head ached, and that you had not slept well. I confess I did not either—not very. Tom and I talked rather late; you know he sails for Liverpool at noon. Sure enough, you didn't know. Well, no matter. The vessel is just about sailing now. Yes, it is *rather* sudden. We talked so much of it last night that it seems quite an old story to me to-day, though. You know he was to go in two weeks, anyway. It seemed best to go earlier, so I helped him pack, and saw him to the steamer two hours ago. You know a man doesn't have to take anything but a tooth-brush and a smoking-cap. We thought it would be best for his health to go at once. Tom has not seemed quite himself of late." She did not look at her friend as she talked and her white face was turned from the light. She talked so fast, it seemed as if she had rehearsed and was repeating a part with a desire to have it over as soon as might be. "His Travelling Ancestor, the one who wants change—change—change in all things, has had hold of him of late. I'm sure you have noticed how restless he was."

The girl sat up and listened with wide eyes and flushed cheeks. She had known many unexpected and unexplained things to be done in the house of this friend, who had given her a home and a warm welcome a year before, when she had left school, an orphan and homeless. But this sudden departure she had not heard even mentioned before. She thought she understood it.

"O Florence! Florence!" she cried, passionately. "It is *my* fault! I have separated you! I have brought sorrow to you! You, who are so good, *so good;* and I—oh, how *can* you be so kind to me? *Hate* me! *Hate me!* Thrust me from your house, and tell the world I tried to steal your husband! Tell that I am vile and wicked! Tell—and now I have sent him away from you, who love him—whom he loves! Why do you not blame me? Why do you never blame anyone? Why—"

There was a pause; the girl sobbed bitterly, while the older woman seemed afraid to trust her voice. After a while in a tired, solemn tone, Nellie went on:

"Do you think you can believe a word I say, Florence? Is there any use for me to tell you the truth?"

Her friend nodded slowly, looking her steadily in the eyes. Her lips were tightly drawn together, and her hands were cold and trembling.

"Then, Florence, I will tell you, truly—truly—truly, as I hope for—" She was going to say "your forgiveness," but it seemed too cruel to ask for that just now. "I did not understand, not at first, either him or myself. I thought he was like you"—she felt Florence shudder—"and loved me, as he said, as you did. I was so glad and proud, until—until—O Florence! how can I tell you that I let him *beg* me to go away with him! After I understood what he meant, my heart *did* leap, even in its utter self-abasement and wretchedness. I let him beg me twice, and kiss me, *after* I understood! It must have been my fault; he said it was"—Florence took her friend's hand in hers—"and he said that no one else had ever taken his thoughts away from you."

The girl thought she saw the drawn lips before her curl; but she must free her whole heart now, and lay bare her very soul.

"He said that he had always been true to you, Florence, even in thought, until I—O Florence! I must be worse than anyone one earth. I—he said—"

Florence Campbell sprang to her feet. "Yes, I know, I know!" she exclaimed, breathlessly, "and you *believed* him! Poor little fool! Women do. Sometimes a second time, but not a third time, dear—not a third time! Do not blame yourself any more." She stopped, then hurried on as one will do when danger threatens from within. "If it had not been you, it would, it might—my God! it might have been worse! Some poor girl—"

She stopped again as if choking. The two women looked at each other; the younger one gave a long, shuddering moan, and buried her face in her hands.

Presently Florence said slowly: "All ancestors were not thieves. Some were simply fickle, and light, and faithless."

Nellie raised a face full of passionate suffering: "Florence! Florence! how can you excuse either of us? How *can*—"

Suddenly, with a great sob, Florence Campbell threw herself into the girl's outstretched arms, and with a wail of utter desolation cried: "Hush, Nellie, hush! Never speak of it again, never! Only *love* me, *love me*—*love me!* I need it so! And *no* one—no one in all the world has ever loved me truly!" It was the only time Nellie ever saw Florence Campbell lose her self-control.

FLORENCE CAMPBELL'S FATE.

"'Tis the good reader that makes the good book; a good head cannot read amiss; in every book he finds passages which seem confidences or asides hidden from all else and unmistakably meant for his ear...."

"Every man has a history worth knowing, if he could tell it, or if we could draw it from him."—Ralph Waldo Emerson.

I was sitting in my office, with my head in my hands, and with both elbows resting on my desk. I was tired in every nerve of my body; more than that, I was greatly puzzled over the strange conduct of my predecessor in the college, whose assistant I had been, and whose place I was appointed to fill during the unexpired term for which he had been elected lecturer on anatomy.

That morning he was to introduce me to the class formally as his successor, deliver his last lecture, and then retire from active connection with anatomical instruction.

Everything appeared to be perfectly arranged, and, indeed, some of the younger men—under my direction—had taken special pains to provide our outgoing and much admired professor with rather unusual facilities for a brilliant close to his career as our instructor.

I was feeling particularly pleased with the arrangements, when, after a neat little speech on his part, commendatory of me, and when we supposed him to be about to begin his lecture, he suddenly turned to me and said, bluntly: "You will be so good as to take the class to-day. Young gentlemen, I bid you good morning," and abruptly took up his hat and left. I sat facing an expectant and surprised class of shrewd young fellows, and I was quite unprepared to proceed.

I had intended my first lecture to be a great success. It was ready for the following day; but my notes were at home, and my position can, therefore, be better imagined than described.

I was thinking over this and the strange behavior of my generally punctilious predecessor, when he entered my office, unannounced, and, after the ordinary salutations and apologies for having placed me in so undesirable a position in the morning, he told me the following episode from his history. I will give it in his own words, omitting, as far as possible, all comment made by me at the time, thus endeavoring to leave you alone with him and his story, as I was that night. This will better enable me to impart the effect to you as it was conveyed to me at the time. It greatly interested me then, but the more

I think it over, the less am I able to decide, in my own mind, all of the psychological questions which it aroused then and which it has since called up. This is the story.

I.

I am, as you know, not a young man, and in the practice of my profession, which has extended over a period of nearly thirty years, I have learned to diagnose the cases that come under my care very slowly and by degrees. Every year has taught me, what you will undoubtedly learn—for I have great hopes for your future career—that physical symptoms are often the results of mental ailments, and that, while cordials and powders are sometimes very useful aids, the first and all-important thing is to understand fully the *true* history of my patient.

I have laid stress upon the word true, simply because while *a* history is easy enough to get, about the most difficult matter in this world to secure is *the* history of one who comes to a physician ailing in body or in mind. It is easy enough to treat a broken leg, a gunshot wound, or even that ghastliest of physical foes, diphtheria, if it is one of these and nothing more.

But if it is a broken leg as to outward sign, and a broken heart as an inward fact, then the case is quite another matter, and the treatment involves skill of a different kind.

If the bullet that tore its way through the body was poisoned with the bitterness of disappointment, anxiety, terror, or remorse, something more is needed than bandages and beef-tea.

If diphtheria was contracted solely from a defective sewage-pipe, it will, no doubt, yield to remedies and pure air. But if long years of nervous and mental prostration have made ready its reception, the work to be done is of a much more serious nature.

So when I was first called to see Florence Campbell, the message conveyed to me threw no light on the case, beyond what the most ordinary observer would have detected at a glance.

The note read thus:

"Dr. H. Hamilton.

"Dear Sir: Although I have been in your city for several months, it is the first time since I came that I have myself felt that I needed medical attention. I have, therefore, not sent you the enclosed note (the history of which you no doubt know) until now. If you will read it, it will explain that the time has now come when, if you will come to me, I need your care.

"Yours respectfully,

"Florence Campbell."

"Parlor 13, F——— Ave. Hotel."

The note enclosed was from a physician in Chicago whom I had known intimately many years before, but with whom, contrary to the hint given by the lady, I had held no communication for a long time past. It said:

"My Dear Doctor: One of my patients is about to visit your city. The length of her stay is uncertain, and, as she is often ailing, she has asked me to give her a note to one whom I believe to be skilful and to possess the qualities which she requires in a physician. In thinking over the list of those known to me in New York, I have decided to give her this note to you. I need not commend her to you; she will do that for herself. You will see at a glance that she is a charming woman, and you will learn in five minutes' conversation with her, that she is a brilliant one. She is also one of those rare patients to whom you can afford to tell the unvarnished truth—an old hobby of yours, I remember—and from whom you can expect it. She has had no serious illness recently, but is rather subject to slight colds and sick headache. I give her sulph. 12. She always responds to that in time.

"Yours, as ever,

"Thomas C. Griswold."

I folded the note and laid it on my desk and took up a pen. Then, on second thought, I turned to the messenger and said, "Say to Miss Campbell that I will call at four o'clock this afternoon."

Before I had finished the sentence he was gone, and I laid down the pen and sat thinking.

How like Tom Griswold that was—the old Tom of college days—to write such a note as that and give it to a patient! "Sulph. 12"—and then I laughed outright at his interpretation of my desire for veracious relations between patient and practitioner, and re-read his note from end to end.

Then I read hers again. Neither of them indicated the slightest need of haste on my part.

I pictured a pretty little blonde—I knew Tom's taste. He had been betrothed to three different girls during the old days, and they had all been of that type; small, blue-eyed, Dresden-china sort of girls, who had each pouted—and married someone else in due time, after a "misunderstanding" with Tom.

One of these misunderstandings had been over some roses, I remember. They did not "match" her dress in color, and she was wretched. She told him he should have known better than to get that shade, when he knew very well that she never wore anything that would "go with" it.

He had naturally felt a little hurt, since he had bought the finest and highest-priced roses to be had, and expected ecstatic praise of his taste and extravagance. The "misunderstanding" was final, and, after a wretched evening and several days of tragic grief, five tinted notes of sorrow, reproach, and pride, they each began to flirt with some one else and to talk of the inconstancy of the other sex. They vowed, of course, that they would never marry anybody on earth, and finally engaged themselves to marry some one else, who perhaps, had just passed through a similar harrowing experience and was yearning to be consoled.

I remember that Tom smoked a great deal during this tragic period, that he looked gloomy, wore only black neckties, and allowed a cold to run on until it became thoroughly settled and had to be nursed all the rest of the winter.

He knew that smoking injured him, and he doubtless had an idea that he would end his misery by means of this cold, supplemented by nicotine poison. How near he might have approached to success it would be difficult to tell, if he had not met my sister Nellie at Christmas-time, and, after having told his woes to her, promised her, "as a friend," not to smoke again for three days and then to report to her. The report was satisfactory, and she then confessed that she had forsworn bonbons for the same length of time, as a sort of companionship in sacrifice.

This, of course, impressed Tom as a truly remarkable test of friendship and sympathy, and,—well, what is the use to tell the rest?

You will know it. It had no new features, so far as I can now recall, and I believe that they had been betrothed six months before Nellie met grave old Professor Menlo and began the study of Greek roots and mythology.

I think that, perhaps, Tom would have been all right if it had not been for the mythology. But Nellie was romantic, and the professor was an enthusiast in this branch of knowledge, and so, by and by, Tom, poor devil, took to smoking again—this time it was a pipe—and local papers were filled with notices of the romantic marriage of "Wisdom and Beauty," and poor little Nellie wrote a pathetic note to Tom, and sent it by me, with frantic directions not to allow him to kill himself because she had not understood her own heart; but that she loved him truly—as a friend—still, and he must come to see her and *her* professor in their new home on the hill. And, dear, dear, what a time I had with Tom! It is funny enough now; but even I felt sorry for him then, and shielded him from the least unnecessary pain by telling the boys that they absolutely must not congratulate me on my sister's marriage, nor mention it in any way whatever, when Tom was present, unless they wanted to have trouble with me personally.

And to think that Tom married Kittie Johnson before he had fairly finished his first year in the hospital service; and had to take her home for his father to support! Since then I had seen him from time to time, and heard of his large practice, his numerous children, and his elegant home; but he never talked of his wife, although I believed him to be perfectly satisfied with her. He seemed content, was prosperous beyond expectation, and had grown fat and gouty, when I last saw him at a medical convention. He attributed his too great flesh and his gout to the climate of his Western home, and was constantly threatening to retire from practice, and said that he should ultimately come to New York to live.

Yes, undoubtedly Florence Campbell is a petite blonde, with little white teeth and a roseleaf cheek, thought I, and I laughed, and rang for my carriage.

II.

I do not know that I ever entered a more delicately perfumed room—and I am very sensitive to perfumes—than the one in which Florence Campbell sat.

She arose from her deep arm-chair as I entered, and, extending her hand, grasped mine with a vigor unusual in a woman, even when she is well.

"This is Dr. Hamilton?" she said, in a clear voice, which told nothing of pain, and was wholly free from the usually querulous note struck by women who are ill, or who think that they are. "This is Dr. Hamilton? I am very glad to see you, doctor. I am Florence Campbell. You received a note from your friend, Dr. Griswold, of Chicago, and one telling how I came to send it to you—how I came into possession of it." Direct of speech, clear of voice, hand feverish, but firm in grasp, I commented mentally, as she spoke.

This is not what I had expected. This is not the limp little blonde that I had pictured, on a lounge, in tears, with the light fluffy hair in disorder, and a tone of voice which plead for sympathy. This is not the figure I had expected to see.

She stood with her back to the light, very erect and well poised.

"Come to the window," I said. "Does your head ache?" That is always a safe question to ask, you know.

She laughed. "Oh, I don't know that it does—not particularly. I fancy there is not enough inside of it to ache much. Mere bone and vacuity could not do a great deal in that line, could it, doctor?" Then she laughed again. She looked me in the eyes, and I fancied she was diagnosing *me*.

Her eyes were deep, large, and brown, or a dark gray; her complexion was dark and clear—almost too transparent; her cheeks were flushed a little; and the light in her eyes was unnaturally intense.

She was evidently trying to gain time—to take my measure.

"It is always a rather trying thing to get a new doctor; don't you think so?" she asked, with another little laugh. "I always feel so foolish to think I have called him to come for so trifling a matter as my ailments are. I am never really ill, you know," she said with nervous haste; "but I am not very strong, and so I often feel—rather—under the weather, and I always fancy that a doctor can prevent, or cure it; but I suppose he cannot. I shall really not expect a great deal of you, in that line, doctor. I cannot expect you to furnish me with robust ancestors, can I? Just so you keep me out of bed"—and here, for the first time, I noticed a slight tremor in her voice—"just keep me so that I can read, and—so that I shall not need to sit alone, and—think—I shall be quite satisfied—quite." She had turned her face away, as she said the last; but I saw that she was having a hard struggle to keep back the tears, notwithstanding the little laugh that followed.

I had felt her pulse; it was hardly perceptible, and fluttered rather than beat; and I had watched her closely as she spoke; but whenever she came near the verge of showing deeper than the surface she broke in with that non-committal little laugh, or turned her face, or half closed her great eyes, and I was foiled. Her pulse and the faint blue veins told me one story; she tried to tell me quite another.

"How are you suffering to-day," I asked.

She looked steadily at me a moment, then lowered her eyes, raised her left hand (upon which I remember noticing there was a handsome ring), looked at its palm a moment, held her lips tightly closed, and then, with a sudden glance at me, again as if on the defensive said:

"I hardly know; I am only a little under the weather; I am weak. I am losing my—grip—on myself; I am—losing my grip—on my—nerves. I cannot afford to do that." The last was said with more emotion than she cared to display. So she arose, walked swiftly to the dressing-case, took up a lace handkerchief, glanced at herself in the mirror, moved a picture (I noticed that it was a likeness of an old gentleman, perhaps her father), and returned to a chair which stood in the shadow, and then, with a merry little peal of laughter, said: "Well, I don't wonder, doctor, that you are unable to diagnose that case. It would require a barometer to do that I fancy, from the amount of weather I got into it. But really, now, how am I to know what is the matter with me? That is for you to say; I am not the doctor. If you tell me it is malaria, as all of you do, I shall be perfectly satisfied—and take your powders with the docility of an infant in arms. I suppose it is malaria, don't you?"

I wanted to gain time—to study her a little. I saw that she was, or had been really ill; ill, that is, in mind if not in body. I fancied that she had succeeded in deceiving Griswold into treating her for some physical trouble which she did not have, or, if she had it, only as a result of a much graver malady.

The right branch may have been found and nipped off from time time when it grew uncomfortably long, but the root, I believed, had not been touched, and, I thought, had not been even suspected by her former physician.

We of the profession, as you very well know, do not always possess that abiding faith in the knowledge and skill of our brethren that we demand and expect from outsiders.

We claim our right to guess over after our associates, and not always to guess the same thing.

I believed that Griswold had not fully understood his former patient. "Sulph. 12," indeed! Then I smiled, and said aloud:

"Dr. Griswold writes me that in such cases as yours he advises sulph. 12—that it has given relief. Do you call yourself a sulphur patient?" I watched her narrowly, and if she did not smile in a satirical way, I was deceived. "Are you out of that remedy? and do you want more of it?" I asked with a serious face.

She did not reply at once. There seemed to be a struggle in her mind as to how much she would let me know. Then she looked at me attentively for a moment, with a puzzled expression, I thought; an unutterably weary look crossed her face. She said, slowly, deliberately: "I have no doubt sulphur will do as well as anything else. Oh! yes—I am decidedly a sulphur patient, no doubt I suppose I have taken several pints of that innocent remedy in my time. A number of physicians have given it to me from time to time. Your friend is not its only devotee. Sulphur and nux—nux and sulphur! I believe they cure anything short of a broken heart, or actual imbecility, do they not, doctor?" She laughed, not altogether pleasantly.

How far would she go and how far would she let me go, with this humbuggery? I looked gravely into her eyes, and said, "Certainly they will do all that, and more. They sometimes hold a patient until a doctor can decide which of those two interesting complaints is the particular one to be treated. In *your* case I am inclined to suspect—the—that it is—*not* imbecility. I shall therefore begin by asking you to be good enough to tell me what it is that affects your heart."

I had taken her wrist in my hand, as I began to speak. My finger was on her pulse. It gave a great bound, and then beat rapidly; and although her face grew a shade paler and her eyes wavered as they tried to look into mine, I knew that I had both surprised and impressed her.

She recovered herself instantly, and made up her mind to hedge still further. "If there is anything the matter with my heart, you are the first to suspect it. My father, however, died of heart disease, and I have—always—hoped that I should—die as suddenly. But I shall not! I shall not! I am so—wiry—so all-enduring. I recover! I always recover!"

She said this passionately, and as if it were a grave misfortune—as if she were very old. I pretended to take it humorously.

"Perhaps at your advanced age your father might have said the same."

She laughed. She saw a loophole, and immediately took it. "Oh, you think I am very young, doctor, but I am not. People always think me younger than I am—at first. I look older when you get used to me. I am nearly thirty."

I was surprised; I had taken her to be about twenty-three.

"In years or in experience?" I said. "Which way do you count your age?"

She got up suddenly again and walked to the dressing-case, then to the window. In doing so she raised her hand to her eyes. It was the hand with the lace handkerchief in it.

"Experience!" she exclaimed; and then, checking herself. "No, people never think me so old—not at first," she said, returning to her chair. "But I suppose I am not too old to be cured with sulph. 12, am I?" Then she laughed her little nervous, quick laugh, and added: "Dear old Dr. Griswold, what faith he must have in 'sulph. 12.' and in his patients. He seems to think that they were made for each other, as it were; and—of course, I am not a doctor—how do I know they were not?"

"Miss Campbell," I said, stepping quickly to her side and surprising her, "you do not need sulphur. You need to be relieved of this strain on your nerves. Make up your mind to tell me your history to-morrow morning—to tell it all; I do not want some fairy-tale. Until then, take these drops to quiet your nerves."

There were tears in her eyes. She did not attempt to hide them. They ran down her cheeks, and she simply closed the lids and let them flow. I took her lace handkerchief and wiped her cheeks. Then I dropped it in her lap, placed the phial on her stand, took up my hat, and left.

III.

But I did not get her story the next day, nor the next, nor the next.

Her tact was perfectly mystifying in its intricacy; her power of evasion marvellous, and her study of me amusing. She grew weaker and more languid every day; but insisted that she had no pain—"nothing upon which to hang a symptom," she would say.

I suggested that refuge of all puzzled doctors—a change.

"A change!" she said, wearily. "A change! Let me see, I have been here nearly five months. I stayed two months in the last place. I was nine days in San Francisco, one year doing the whole of Europe, and seven months in Asia. Yes, decidedly, I must need a change. There are three places left for me to try, which one do you advise?" There was a bitter little laugh, but her expression was sweet, and her eyes twinkled as she glanced at me.

"I am glad I have three places to choose from," I said. "I was afraid you were not going to leave so many as that, and had already begun to plan 'electric treatment' as a final refuge."

She laughed nervously, but I thought I saw signs of a mental change.

I had always found that I could do most with her by falling into her own moods of humor or merry satire upon her own condition or upon the various stages of medical ignorance and pretence into which we are often driven.

"Where are these three unhappy places that you have so shamelessly neglected? Was it done in malice? I sincerely hope, for their sakes, that it was not so bad as that—that it was a mere oversight on your part," I went on.

"Australia has been spared my presence so far through malice; the other two, through defective theology. I dislike the idea of one of them on account of the climate, and of the other, because of the stupid company," she said, with a droll assumption of perplexity; "so, you see, I can't even hope for a pleasant change after death. Oh, my case is quite hopeless, I assure you, doctor; *quite!*" She laughed again.

I had her where I wanted her now. I thought by a little adroitness I might get, at least, a part of the truth.

"So you are really afraid to die, and yet think that you must," I said, bluntly.

She turned her great luminous eyes on me, and her lip curled slightly, with real scorn, before she forced upon her face her usual mask of good-humored sarcasm.

"Afraid!" she exclaimed, "afraid to die! afraid of what, pray? I cannot imagine being afraid to die. It is *life* I am afraid of. If I could only—" This last passionately. She checked herself abruptly, and with an evident effort resumed her usual light air and tone. "But it does always seem so absurdly impossible to me, doctor, to hear grownup people talk about being afraid to die. It almost surprised me into talking seriously, a reprehensible habit I never allow myself. A luxury few can afford, you know. It skirts too closely the banks of Tragedy. One is safer on the high seas of Frivolity—don't you think?"

"Much safer, no doubt, my child," said I, taking her hand, which was almost as cold and white as marble; "much safer from those deceived and confiding persons who prescribe 'sulph. 12' for the broken heart and overwrought nerves of a little woman who tries bravely to fly her gay colors in the face of defeat and to whistle a tune at a grave."

I had called late, and we were sitting in the twilight, but I saw tears fall on her lap, and she did not withdraw her hand, which trembled violently.

I had touched the wound roughly—as I had determined to do—but, old man as I was, and used to the sight of suffering as I had been for years, I could restrain myself only by an effort from taking her in my arms and asking her to forget what I had said. She seemed so utterly shaken. We sat for some moment in perfect silence, except for her quick, smothered little sobs, and then she said, passionately:

"Oh, my God! doctor, how did you know?" And then, with a flash of fear in her voice, "Who told you? No one has talked me over to you? No one has written to you?"

"I know nothing, except what I have seen of your brave fight, my child. All the information I have had about you, from outside, was contained in that valuable little note of introduction from Griswold."

In spite of her tears and agitation she smiled, but looked puzzled, as I afterward recalled she always did when I mentioned his name, or spoke as if she knew him well.

"I have not watched you for nothing. And I never treat a patient without first diagnosing his case. I do not say that I am *always* right. I am not vain of the methods nor of the progress of my profession; but I am, at least, not blind, and I have always been interested in you. I should like to help you, if you will let me. I can do nothing for you in the dark." Then dropping my voice, significantly: "Does *he* know where you are? Does *he* know you are ill?"

There was a long silence. I did not know but that she was offended. She was struggling for command of her voice, and for courage. Presently she said, in a hoarse whisper, which evidently shocked her as much as it startled me, so unnatural did it sound:

"Who? My husband?"

"Your *husband!*" I exclaimed. "Are you—is there—I did not know you were married. Why did you always allow me to call you *Miss* Campbell?"

"I do not know," she said, wearily. "It made no difference to me, and it seemed to please your fancy to treat me as a child.. But I never really noticed that you did always call me Miss. If I had, I should not have cared. What difference could it make to me—or to you—what prefix you put to my name?"

"But I did not know you were married," I said almost sharply.

She looked up, startled for a moment; but recovering, as from some vague suspicion, in an instant she said, smiling a little, and with evident relief, plunging into a new opening:

"That had nothing to do with my case. There was no need to discuss family relations. I never thought of whether *you* were married or not. You were my doctor—I your patient. What our family relations, wardrobes, or political affiliations might be seem to me quite aside from that. We may choose to talk of them together, or we may not, as the case may be. And in my case, it would not be—edifying." There was a moment's pause, then she said, rather impatiently, but as if the new topic were a relief to her: "The idea that a woman must be ticketed as married or unmarried, to every chance acquaintance, is repellent to me. Men are not so ticketed—and that is right. It is vulgar to suppose a sign is needed to prevent trespass, or to tempt approach. 'Miss Jones, this is Mr. Smith.' What does it tell?" She was talking very rapidly now—nervously. "It tells her, 'Here is a gentleman to whom I wish to introduce you. If you find him agreeable you will doubtless learn more of him later on.' It tells him, 'Here is a lady. *She is not married.* Her family relations—her most private affairs—are thrust in his face before she has even said good evening to him. I think it is vulgar, and it is certainly an unnecessary personality. What his or her marital relations may be would seem to come a good deal later in the stage of acquaintance, don't you think so, doctor?" She laughed, but it was not like herself. Even the laugh had changed. She was fighting for time.

"It is a new idea to me," I said, "and I confess I like it. Come to think of it, it *is* a trifle premature—this thrusting a title intended to indicate private relations onto a name used on all public occasions. By Jove! it is absurd. I never thought of it before; but it is *never* done with men, is it? 'General,' 'Mr.' 'Dr.'—none of them. All relate to him as an individual, leaving vast fields of possibilities all about him. 'Mrs.' 'Miss'—they tell one thing, and one only.

That is of a private nature—a personal association. You have started me on a new line of thought, and," said I, taking her hand again, "you have given me so much that is new to think of to-night that I will go home to look over the budget. You are tired out. Go to bed now. Order your tea brought up. Here is an order to see to anything you may ask, promptly. Beesley, the manager, is an old friend of mine. Any order you may give, if you send it down with this note from me, will be obeyed at once. I shall come to-morrow. Good-night."

I put the order on the table, at her side. I know my voice was husky. It startled me, as I heard it. She sat perfectly still, but she laid her other hand on top of mine, with a light pressure, and her voice sounded tired and full of tears.

"Good-night. You are very kind—very thoughtful. I will be brave to-morrow. Good-night." That night I drove past and saw a light in her window at one o'clock. "Poor child!" I said; "will she be brave enough to tell me to-morrow, or will she die with her burden, and her gay little laugh on her lips?"

IV.

The next day I called earlier than usual. I had spent an almost sleepless night, wondering what I could do for this beautiful, lovable woman, who seemed to be all alone in the world, and who evidently felt that she must remain apart and desolate.

What had caused her to leave her husband? Or had he left her? What for? What kind of a man was he? Did she love him, and was she breaking her heart for him? or did he stand between her and some other love? Had she married young, and made a mistake that was eating her life out? Whose fault was it? How could I help her?

All these and a thousand other questions forced themselves upon me, and none of the answers came to fit the case. Answers there were in plenty, but they were not for these questions nor for this woman—not for this delicate flower of her race.

As I stepped into the hotel office to send my card to "Parlor 13," as was my custom, the clerk looked up with his perfunctory smile and said, "Go' morning, doctor. Got so in the habit 'coming here lately, s'pose it'll take quite a while to taper off. That about the size of it?"

I stared at the young man in utter bewilderment.

"Ha! ha! ha! I believe you'd really forgot already she'd gone;" and then, with a quick flash of surprise and intelligent, detective shrewdness, "You knew she was going, doctor? She did not skip her little bill, did she? Of course not. Her husband was in such a deuce of a hurry to catch the early train, the night-clerk said he was ringing his bell the blessed night for fear they'd get left. Front! take water to 273. You hadn't been gone five minutes last night, when he came skipping down here with your check and order, and we just had to make things hum to get cash enough together to meet it for her; but we made it, and so they got off all right."

"Have you got my check here yet?" asked I, in in a tone that arrested the attention of the other clerk, who looked up in surprise.

"Good heavens! no. Do you think we're made of ready money, just because you are? That check was in the bank and part of the cash in that desk the first thing after banking hours," said he, opening out the register and reaching for a bunch of pens behind him. "You see it cleaned us out last night. I couldn't change two dollars for a man this morning. I told Campbell last night that you must think hotels were run queer, to expect us to cash a five-thousand dollar check on five minutes' notice. Couldn't 'a' done it at all if 't hadn't been pay-night for servants and the rest of us. We all had to wait till to-day. But the old man'll tell you. Here he comes."

"Why, hello! doctor, old boy," said Beesley, coming up from behind and clapping me vigorously on the shoulder. "Didn't expect to see the light of your countenance around here again so soon. Thought we owed it all to your professional ardor for that charming patient of yours up in 13. They got off all right, but if any other man but you had sent that order and check down here for us to cash last night I'd have told him to make tracks. Of course, I understood that they were called away suddenly—unexpectedly, and all that. He told me all about it, and that you did not finish the trade till the last minute; but—"

"*Trade?*" gasped I, in spite of my determination to hear all before disclosing anything. "Trade?"

"Oh, come off. Don't be so consumedly skittish about the use of English, I suppose you want me to say that the 'transaction between you was not concluded,' etc., etc. Oh, you're a droll one, doctor." He appeared to notice a change on my face, which he evidently misconstrued, and he added, gayly. "Oh, it was all right, my boy, as long as it was you—glad to do you a good turn any day; but what a queer idea for that little woman to marry such a man! How did it happen? I'd like to know the history! Every time I saw him come swelling around I made up mind to ask you about them, and then I always forgot it when I saw you. When he told me you had been his wife's guardian I thought some of kicking you the next good chance I got, for allowing the match, and for not telling me you had such a pretty ward. You always were a deep rascal—go off!" He rattled on.

Several times I had decided to speak, but as often restrained myself. My blank face and unsettled manner appeared to touch his sense of humor. He concluded that it was good acting. I decided to confirm the mistake, until I had time to think it all over. Finally, I said, as carelessly as I could:

"How long had this—a—husband been here? That is—when did he get back?"

"Been here! get back! Been here all the time; smoked more good cigars and surrounded more wine than any other one man in the house. Oh, he was a Jim-dandy of a fellow for a hotel!" Then, with sudden suspicion: "Why? Had he told you he'd go away before? Oh! I—see! *That* was the trade? Paid him to skip, hey? M—m—m—yes! I think I begin to catch on." He could hardly restrain his mirth, and winked at me in sheer ecstasy.

I went slowly out. When I arrived at the house I directed the servant to say to anyone who might call that the doctor was not at home. I went to my room and wrote to Dr. Griswold, asking him for information about Florence Campbell, the fair patient he had sent me. "Who was she? What did he know of her? Where were her friends?" I told him nothing of this last development, but asked for an immediately reply, adding—"for an important reason."

Three days later a telegram was handed to me as I drove up to my office. It was this:

"Never heard of her. Why? Griswold?"

I did not sleep that night. For the first time my faith in Florence Campbell wavered. Up to that time I had blamed her husband for everything. I had woven around her a web of plausible circumstances which made her the unwilling victim of a designing villain—an expert forger, no doubt, who used her, without her own knowledge, as a decoy—a man of whom she was both ashamed and afraid, but from whom she could not escape.

But how was all that to be reconciled with this revelation? Griswold did not know her. How about his introduction and that "sulph. 12"? I looked through my desk for Griswold's note. It was certainly his handwriting; but I noticed, for the first time, that it did not mention her name.

Perhaps this was a loop-hole through which I might bring my fair patient— in whom I was beginning to fear I had taken too deep an interest—without discredit to herself.

Might she not have changed her name since Griswold treated her? I determined to give her the benefit of this doubt until I could be sure that it had no foundation.

I felt relieved by this respite, and, heartily ashamed of the unjust suspicion of the moment before, I gave no hint of it in the letter I now wrote Griswold, describing the lady, and in which I enclosed his letter of introduction to me.

The next few days I went about my practice in a dream, and it was no doubt due to fortuitous circumstances rather than to my skill that several of my patients still live to tell the tale of their suffering and of my phenomenal ability to cope with disease in all its malignant power.

V.

In due time Griswold's letter came. I went into my office to read it. I told myself that I had no fears for the good name of Florence Campbell. I knew that some explanation would be made that would confirm me in my opinion of her; but, for all that, I locked the door, and my hand was less steady than I liked to see it, as I tore the end of the envelope.

I even remember thinking vaguely that I usually took time to open my letters with more precision and with less disregard for the untidy appearance of their outer covering afterward. I hesitated to read beyond the first line, although I had so hastened to get that far. I read: "My dear old friend," and then turned the letter over to see how long it was—how much probable information it contained. There were four closely written pages. I wondered if it could all be about Florence Campbell, and was vaguely afraid that it was—and that it was *not*. I remembered looking at the clock when I came into the office. It was nearly six o'clock. I laid the letter down and went to the cooler and got out a bottle of Vichy. I sat it and (placed) some wine by my elbow on the desk, and took up the letter.

"I never heard of anyone by the name of Florence Campbell, so far as I can recall. I certainly never had a patient by that name. Some months ago I gave the letter you enclose—which I certainly did write—to a patient of mine who was on her way to Europe and expected to stay some time in New York on her way through.

"She, however, was in no way like the lady you describe. Her name was Kittie Hatfield, and she was small, with dreamy blue eyes and flaxen hair—a *perfect* woman, in fact." Oh! Tom! Tom! thought I—true to your record, to the last! I had long since ceased to wonder at the lapse, however, for Florence Campbell herself was surely sufficient explanation of all that. "I understood"—the letter went on—"that Kittie did not stop but a few days in New York, when she was joined by the party with which she was to travel. She stayed at the F——— Avenue Hotel, I have learned, and became intimate with some queer people there—much to the indignation of her brother, when he learned of it."

I laid the letter down and put my head on my arms, folded as they were on the desk. I was dizzy and tired. When I raised my head it was dark. I got up, lighted the gas, and found myself stiff and as if I had been long in a forced and unnatural position. I recalled that I had been indignant.

This brother of the silly-pated, blue-eyed girl had not liked her to know Florence Campbell, indeed! He was, no doubt, a precious fool—naturally would be, with such a sister, I commented mentally. What else, I wondered, had Griswold found out? Was the rest of this old fool's letter about her? I began where I had left off.

"I have since learned from him that the man—whose name *was* Campbell—was a foreigner of some kind, with a decidedly vague, not to say, hazy reputation, and that his wife, who was supposed to be an invalid, and an American of good family, never appeared in public, and so was never seen by him—that is by Will Hatfield—but was only known to him through Kittie's enraptured eyes. She was said to be bright and pretty. Kittie is the most generous child alive in her estimate of other women; however, he thinks it possible that Kittie either gave her the letter from me to you, and asked her to have proper medical care, or else that the woman, or her husband, got hold of it in a less legitimate way; which I think quite likely. Kittie thought the Campbell woman was charming." The "Campbell woman," indeed! I felt like a thief, even to read such rubbish, and I should have enjoyed throttling the whole ill-natured gossiping set—not omitting flaxen-haired Kittie herself.

I determined to finish the letter, however.

"Hatfield is so ashamed of his sister's friendship for the woman that I had the utmost difficulty in making him tell me the whole truth, but, from what I gathered yesterday, he thinks them most likely the head of a gang of counterfeiters or forgers and—"

I read no further, or, if I did, I can recall only that. It was burned into my brain, and when a loud pounding on my office-door aroused me, I found the letter twisted and torn into a hundred pieces, the Vichy and wine-bottles at my side half-empty, and the hands of the clock pointing to half-past ten.

"Doctor, doctor," called my lackey; "oh, doctor! Oh, lord, I'm afraid something's wrong with the doctor, but I'm afraid to break in the door."

I went to the door to prevent a scene. One of my best patients stood there, with Morgan, the man. Both of them were pale and full of suppressed excitement.

"Heavens and earth, doctor, we were afraid you were dead. I've been waiting here a good hour for you to come home. No one knew you were in, till Morgan peeped over the transom. What in the devil is the matter?" said my patient.

"Tired out, went to sleep," said I; but I did not know my own voice as I spoke. It sounded distant, and its tones were strange.

They both looked at me suspiciously, and with evident anxiety as to my mental condition. I caught at the means of escape.

"I am too tired to see anyone to-night. In fact, I am not well. You will have to let me off this time. Get Dr. Talbott, next door, if anyone is sick; I am going to bed. Good-night."

There was a long pause. Then he said, wearily: "You are a young man, doctor. You have taken the chair I left vacant at the college. I would never have told the story to you, perhaps, only I wanted you to know why I left the class in your care so suddenly this morning, when I uncovered the beautiful face of the 'subject' you had brought from the morgue for me to give my closing lecture upon. That class of shallow-pated fellows have not learned yet that doctors—even old fellows like me—know a good deal less than they think they do about the human race—themselves included."

I stammered some explanation of the circumstances, and again there was a long silence.

Then he said:

"Found drowned, was she? Poor girl! Do you believe, with that face, she was ever a bad woman? Or that she had anything to do with the rascality of her husband, even if he were consciously a rascal? and who is to judge of that, knowing so little of him? Did I ever recover the five thousand dollars? Did I attempt to recover it? Oh, no. All this happened nearly ten years ago now; and if that were all it had cost me I should not mind. The hotel people never knew. Why should they? This is the first time I have told the story. You think I am an old fool? Well, well, perhaps I am—perhaps I am; who can say what any of us are, or what we are not? Thirty years ago I knew that I understood myself and everybody else perfectly. To-day I know equally well that I understand neither the one nor the other. We learn that fact, and then we die—and that is about all we do learn. You wonder, after what I tell you, if the beautiful face at the demonstration class this morning was really hers, or whether a strong likeness led my eyes and nerves astray You wonder if she drowned herself, and why? Was it an accident? Did *he* do it? This last will be decided by each one according as he judges of Florence Campbell and her husband—of who and what they were. Perhaps I shall try to find him now. Not for the money, but to learn why she married the man he seemed to be. It is hard to tell what I should learn. It is not even easy to know just what I should *like* to learn; and perhaps, after all, it is better not to know more—who shall say?"

And the doctor bade me good-night and bowed himself out to his carriage with his old courtesy, and left me alone with the strange, sad story of the beautiful girl whose lifeless form had furnished the subject of my first lecture to a class of medical students.

MY PATIENTS STORY.

"Things are cruel and blind; their strength detains and deforms:
And the wearying wings of the mind still beat up the stream of their storms.
Still, as one swimming up stream, they strike out blind in the blast.
In thunders of vision and dream, and lightning of future and past.
We are baffled and caught in the current, and bruised upon edges of shoals;
As weeds or as reeds in the torrent of things are the wind-shaken souls."

Algernon Charles Swinburne.

I.

Perhaps I may have told you before, that at the time of which I speak, my Summer home—where I preferred to spend much more than half of the year—was on a sandy beach a few miles out of New York, and also that I had retired from active practice as a physician, even when I was in the city.

Notwithstanding these two facts, I was often called in consultation, both in and out of the city; and was occasionally compelled to take a case entirely into my own hands, through some accident or unforeseen circumstance.

It was one of these accidents which brought the patient whose story I am about to tell you, under my care.

I can hardly say now, why I retained the case instead of turning it over to some brother practitioner, as was my almost invariable habit; but for some reason I kept it in my own hands, and, as it was the only one for which I was solely responsible at the time, I naturally took more than ordinary interest in and paid more than usual attention to all that seemed to me to bear upon it.

As you know I am an "old school" or "regular" physician, although that did not prevent me from consulting with, and appreciating the strong points of many of those who were of other, and younger branches of the profession.

This peculiarity had subjected me, in times gone by, to much adverse criticism from some of my colleagues who belonged to that rigidly orthodox faction which appears to feel that it is a much better thing to allow a patient to die "regularly"—as it were—than it is to join forces with one, who, being of us, is still not with us in theory and practice.

Recognizing that we were all purblind at best, and that there was and still is, much to learn in every department of medicine, it did not always seem to me that it was absolutely necessary to reject, without due consideration, the guesses of other earnest and careful men, even though they might differ from me in the prefix to the "pathy" which forms the basis of the conjecture.

We are all wrong so often that it has never appeared to be a matter of the first importance—it does not present itself to my mind as absolutely imperative—that it should be invariably the same wrong, or that all of the mistakes should necessarily follow the beaten track of the "old school."

I had arrived at that state of beatitude where I was not unwilling for a life to be saved—or even for pain to be alleviated, by other methods than my own.

I do not pretend that this exalted ethical status came to me all at once, nor at a very early stage of my career; but it came, and I had reaped the whirlwind of wrath, as I have just hinted to you.

So when my patient let me know, after a time, that he had been used to homeopathic treatment, I at once suggested that he send for some one of that school to take charge of his case.

He declined—somewhat reluctantly, I thought, still, quite positively. But, in the course of events, when I felt that a consultation was due to him as well as to myself, I asked him if he would not prefer that the consulting physician should be of that school.

He admitted that he would, and I assured him that I should be pleased to send for any one he might name.

He knew no doctor here, he said, and left it to me to send for the one in whom I had the greatest confidence.

It is at this point my story really begins.

I stopped on my way uptown to arrange, with Dr. Hamilton, of Madison Avenue, a consultation that afternoon, at three o'clock. I told the doctor all that I, myself, knew at that time, of my patient's history. Three weeks before I had been in a Fifth Avenue stage; a gentleman had politely arisen to offer his seat to a lady at the moment that the stage gave a sudden lurch which threw them both violently against each other and against the end of the stage.

He broke the fall for her; but he received a blow on the head, which member came in contact with the money-box, with a sharp crack. Accustomed to the sight of pain and suffering as I was, the sound of the blow and his suddenly livid face gave me a feeling of sickness which did not wholly leave me for an hour afterward. Involuntarily I caught him in my arms—he was a slightly built man—and directed the driver to stop at the first hotel.

The gentleman was unconscious and I feared he had sustained a serious fracture of the skull. He was evidently a man of culture, and I thought not an American. I therefore wished, if possible, to save him a police or hospital experience.

By taking him into the first hotel I reasoned, we could examine him; learn who and what he was, where he lived, and, after reviving him, send him home in a carriage.

The process of bringing him back to consciousness was slow, and as the papers on his person, which we felt at liberty to examine, gave no clue to his residence, we concluded to put him to bed and trust to farther developments to show us what to do in the matter of removal. The lady on whose account he had received the injury had given me her card, which bore a name well known on the Avenue, and had stated that she would, if necessary, be responsible for all expense at the hotel.

It was deemed best, therefore, to put him to bed, as I said before, and wait for him to indicate, for himself, the next move. I placed in the safe of the hotel his pocketbook, which contained a large sum of money (large that is, for a man to carry on his person in these days of cheques and exchanges) and his watch, which was a handsome one, with this inscription on the inside cover, "T. C. from Florence."

The cards in his pocket bore different names and addresses, mostly foreign, but the ones I took for his own were finely engraved, and read "Mr. T. C. Lathro," nothing more. No address, no business; simply calling cards, of a fashionable size, and of the finest quality.

This, as I say, was about three weeks before I concluded to call Dr. Hamilton in consultation; and I had really learned very little more of my patient's affairs than these facts taken from his pocket that first day while he was still unconscious.

He was silent about himself, and while he had slowly grown better his progress toward health did not satisfy me, nor do I think that he was wholly of opinion, that I was doing quite all that should be done to hasten his recovery.

He was always courteous, self-poised, and able to bear pain bravely; but I thought he watched me narrowly, and I several times detected him in a weary sigh and an impatient movement of the eyebrows, which did not tally with his assumption of cheerful indifference and hospitality.

I use the word hospitality advisedly, for his effort always seemed to be to treat me as a guest whom he must entertain, and distract from observing his ailments, rather than as a physician whose business it was to discover and remedy them.

He had declined to be moved; said he was a stranger; had no preferences as to hotels; felt sure this one was as comfortable as any; thanked me over and over for having taken him there, and changed the subject. He would talk as long as I would allow him on any subject, airily, brightly, readily. On any subject, that is, except himself; yet from his conversation I had gathered that he had travelled a great deal; was a man of wealth and culture, whether French, Italian or Russian, I could not decide. He spoke all of these languages, and words from each fitted easily into place when for a better English one, he hesitated or was at a loss.

Indeed, he seemed to have seen much of every country and to have observed impartially—without national prejudice. He knew men well, too well to praise recklessly; and he sometimes gave me the impression, I can hardly say how, that blame was a word whose meaning he did not know.

He spoke of having seen deeds of the most appalling nature in Russia, and talked of their perpetrators sometimes, as good and brave men. He never appeared to measure men by their exceptional acts.

Occasionally I contested these points with him, and I am not sure but that it may have been the interest I took in his conversation that held me as his physician; for as I said, I was well aware that he did not improve as he should have done after the first few days.

But I liked to hear him talk. He was a revelation to me. I greatly enjoyed his breath and charity—if I may so express the mental attitude which recognized neither the possession of, nor the need for, either quality in his judgments of his fellow-men.

He had evidently not been able to pass through life under the impression that character, like cloth, is cut to fit a certain outline, and that after the basting-threads are once in, no farther variation need be looked for. Indeed, I question if he would have been able to comprehend the mental condition of those grown-up "educated" children who are never able to outgrow the comfortable belief that words and acts have a definite, inflexible, par-value—that an unabridged dictionary, so to speak, is an infallible appeal; who, in short, expect their villains to be consistently and invariably villainous, in the regulation orthodox fashion.

Individual shades of meaning, whether of language or of character, do not enter into their simple philosophy. Mankind suffers, in their pennyweight scales, a shrinkage that is none the less real because they never suspect that the dwarfage may be due to themselves—to their system of weights and measures. All variations from their standard indicate an unvarying tendency to mendacity. He whom they once detect in a quibble, or in an attempt to acquire the large end of a bargain, never recovers (what is perhaps only his rightful heritage, in spite of an occasional lapse) the respect and confidence of these primer students who are inflexible judges of all mental and moral manifestations.

I repeat that this comfortable and regular philosophy was foreign to my patient's mental habits, and I began to consider, the more I talked with him, that it did not agree with my own personal observations. I reflected that I was not very greatly surprised, nor did I lose faith in a man necessarily, when I discovered him in a single mean or questionable action.

Why, then, should I be surprised to find those of whom I had known only ill-engaged in deeds of the most unselfish nature? Deeds of heroism and generosity such as he often recounted as a part of the life of some of these same terrible Russian officials. There seems, however, to be that in us which finds it far easier to reconcile a single mean or immoral action with an otherwise upright life, than to believe it likely, or even possible, for a depraved nature to perform, upon occasion, deeds of exalted or unusual purity. Yet so common is the latter, that its failure of recognition by humanity in general can be due it seems to me, only to a wrong teaching or to a stupidity beyond even normal bounds.

For, after all, the bad man who is all bad, is really a less frequent product than that much talked of, but rare creature, a perfect woman. Perhaps one could count the specimens of either of these to be met with in a life time, on the fingers of one hand.

But to return to my patient and his story.

It was of these things that he and I had often talked, and I had come to greatly respect the self-poise and acute observation, as well as the broad human sympathy of this reserved and evidently sad-hearted man. Sad-hearted I knew, in spite of his keen sense of humor, and his firm grasp of philosophy.

I gave Dr. Hamilton a brief outline of all this, as well as of the physical condition of the man whom he was to see; for I believe it to be quite as important for a physician to understand and diagnose the mental as the physical conditions of those who come under his care before he can prescribe intelligently for other than very trifling ailments.

You can imagine my surprise when I tell you that the moment Dr. Hamilton stepped into the room, and I mentioned his name, my patient, this self-poised man of the world, whose nerves had often seemed to me to be of tempered steel, looked up suddenly as you have seen a timid child do when it is sharply reproved, and fainted dead away.

II.

I confess that I expected a scene.

I glanced at the doctor, but he showed no sign of ever having seen my patient before, and went to work with me in the most methodical and indifferent way possible to revive him.

"You did not mention that this was one of his symptoms—a peculiarity of his. Has he been subject to this sort of thing? Did he say he was subject to it before he hurt his head, or has it developed since?" the doctor inquired quietly as we worked.

I bit my lip. His tone was so exasperatingly cool, while, knowing my patient as I did, his startled manner and sudden fainting had impressed me deeply.

"It is the first time," I said, "since he was hurt—that is, since he recovered consciousness after the blow—that he has exhibited the slightest tendency to anything of the kind."

I hesitated, then I said: "Doctor, if you know him; if this is the result of seeing you suddenly (for he did not know who was to come) don't you think— would it be well?—Do you think it best for you to be where he will see you when he begins to revive?"

The doctor stared at me, then at my patient. "I don't know him—never saw him before in my life so far as I know. What did you say his name is? Mum— oh, yes, Lathro—first and only time I ever heard it. Oh, no, I suppose his nerves are weak. The excitement of seeing me—the idea of—a—er— consultation." I smiled, involuntarily. "You don't know the man, doctor," said I. "He is bomb proof as to nerves in that sense of the word. He—a— There must be some other reason. He must have mistaken you for some one else. I am sorry to trouble you, doctor, but would you kindly step into the other room? He will open his eyes now, you see."

When, a moment later, my patient regained consciousuess, he glanced about him furtively, like a hunted man. He did not look like himself.

He examined my face closely—suspiciously, I thought—for a moment. Then I laughed lightly, and said: "Well, old fellow, you've been trying your hand at a faint. That's a pretty way to treat a friend. I come in to see you; you step out to nobody knows where—to no man's land—and give me no end of trouble rowing you back to our shore. What did you eat for dinner that served you that kind of a trick?"

He looked all about the room again, examined my face, and then smiled, for the first time since I had known him, nervously, and said:

"I think my digestion must be pretty badly out of order. I'll declare I saw double when you came in. I thought there were two of you; and the other one—wasn't you."

I laughed; "That is good. Two of me, but the other one wasn't me. Well, thank heaven there is only one of me up to date."

He smiled, but seemed disturbed still. I decided to ask him a direct question:

"Well now, just suppose there had been two of me—is that an excuse for you to faint? Does associating with one of me try you to that extent that two of me would prostrate you?"

He did not take me up with his old manner. He was listless and absent. I said that I would go down to the office and order some wine and return at once. I slipped into the other room, and with my finger on my lips motioned to Dr. Hamilton to pass out quietly before me.

I followed him. "There is something wrong, Doctor," I said: "I am sorry, but I shall have to ask you to go without seeing him again. I can't tell you why yet, but I'll try to find out and let you know. Order some champagne sent up to me, please, as you go out, and I will see you as soon as I can."

The moment I re-entered the room, my patient, whose restless eyes met mine as I opened the door, said: "I thought you were talking to some one."

"I was," said I carelessly; a bell-boy, "I ordered wine. It will be up soon." Then I changed the subject; but he was nervous and unlike himself and none of the old topics interested him.

When the door opened for the boy with the wine an expression of actual terror passed over my patient's face. When I left him a half hour later I was puzzled and anxious.

III.

The moment I entered his room on the following day he said: "I thought you had planned to have another doctor come and look me over, yesterday." He was watching me closely as he spoke: "Did I hear you mention his name?"

Ah, thought I, here *is* a mystery in spite of Dr. Hamilton's denial. I will try him.

"Yes," I said, "I had decided to ask the best Homeopathic doctor I know, a skilful man, especially successful in diagnosing cases, to overhaul you and see if he agrees with me that you ought to be on your feet this blessed minute, if my diagnosis of your case is entirely right. I don't see why you are still so weak. He may find the spring that I have missed. Why?"

"Did you—I am not acquainted with the doctors here,—I think you said his name is—?"

"I have not mentioned his name to you," I said, "but the one I had in mind is Dr. Hamilton of—— Madison Avenue."

There was no doubt about it, the color rose slowly to his face, and he was struggling for self-control. At length he said: "No, I do not wish to see another doctor. I am perfectly satisfied with you. I am—I say—no, positively do not ask him; that is, do not ask anyone to come unless I know and definitely agree to it. And I certainly shall want to know who he is first."

All this was wholly foreign to the man, to his nature and habit.

"Tell me," I said, "what you have against Dr. Hamilton, for I cannot fail to see that there is something behind all this."

He did not reply for some time; then he said wearily, but with great depth of feeling.

"I suppose I may as well tell you. I cannot forgive him for an injury I did him long ago."

I did not say anything nor did I look at him. Presently he went on hoarsely; "If I had only injured him, perhaps I could get over it but I took a mean advantage of—I did it through a woman who liked him—and whom he— loved and trusted." There was another long silence; then I said; "You were right to tell me, Lathro. You need not fear that I will betray you to him, and he does not know you. He did not recognize you either before or after you fainted. Of course I knew there was something wrong. He will not come again."

He sprang to his feet, and a wave of red surged into his face. "I knew it! I knew I had seen him! I was sure it was not a delusion," he said. "He was here.

No, he would not know me. He never saw me. I did not injure him like a man, I struck from behind a woman. A woman who cared for his respect, and I let him blame her. I suppose I could get over it if it were not for that. I came back here partly to let him know, if I could some way, that she was not to blame"—there was another long silence—"and partly to get rid of myself. Russia did not do it,—Turkey,—France—none of them. I thought perhaps he would—I had some sort of a wild idea that he might settle with me some way. I have carried that forged cheque in my brain, until—"

I started visibly. I had had no idea that it was so bad as this. I changed my position to hide or cover the involuntary movement I had made, but he had seen it and the color died out of his face. He forced himself to begin again. "I carried that forged check," he was articulating now with horrible distinctness, "wherever I went. She never knew anything about it. She knew I was—she thought, or feared, that I might be somewhat—what you Americans call crooked; but she did not know the truth, not until the very last. She knew that I had been unreliable in some ways long ago; but she did not dream of the worst. At last,—sometimes I think I was a fool to have done it,—but I told her. I told her the whole truth, and—she left me. She had borne everything till then. I think she came here. Before long I followed. She told me not to, and I said I would not; but of course I did. I could not help it. I knew then, and I know now, that I am putting myself into the clutches of the law; but I do not care—not now— since I cannot find Florence Campbell."

He pronounced the name as if it were a treasure wrung from him by force. "It is the only really criminal thing I ever did. I do not know why I did it. They say that crime—a taste for it, develops slowly, by degrees. Maybe so; but not with me, not with me.

"I had money enough; but—oh, my God! how I hated him. I saw that he was growing to love her without knowing it. I often heard them talking together. They did not know it, and if they had it could not have been more innocent; but I was madly jealous, for the first time in my life. I determined to make him think ill of her, and yet I said just now that forgery was my only crime. That was worse, by far, but I believe it is not a crime in law."

He smiled scornfully. "I have outgrown all that now. The storm has left me the wreck you see; but I thought it all out last night, and determined to tell you. You are to tell—him—for her sake," he said between his set teeth.

"He may see her yet some day. She will never return to me—God bless her! God help us both!"

"No, she will never return to you nor to anyone else," I said, as gently as I could.

He sprang up with the energy of a maniac. "How do you know? What do you know?" he demanded.

"I only know that she is dead, my friend," I said, placing my hand on his arm, "and that Dr. Hamilton does not wish to punish you. I heard it all; the story of the forgery of his name, and that a Florence Campbell was in some way connected with it. I heard it from him long, long ago; but he does not know that you are Tom Campbell. You are safe."

"Does not wish to punish me! I am safe! Great God, no one could punish me. I do that. Safe! Oh, the irony of language!"

There was a long pause. He had gone to the window and was staring out into the darkness.

Presently the sound of convulsive sobbing filled the room; I thought best to remain near the door and make no effort to check his grief with words.

At last the storm spent itself. He came slowly into the middle of the room and stood facing me. At length he said:

"One of the greatest punishments is gone, thank God. Florence Campbell is dead, you say. Do you know what it is, Doctor, to wish that one you loved was dead?"

"Yes, yes." I said; "but it is best for you not to talk any more—nor think, just now—not of that—not of that."

He broke in impatiently—"Don't you know me well enough yet to know that that sort of thing—that sort of professional humbug is useless? Must not talk more of that—nor think of it, indeed! What else do you suppose I ever think of? The good men who are bad and the bad ones who are good—the puppets of our recent conversations? Suppose we boil it down a little. Am I a bad man? That is a question that puzzles me. Am I a good one? At least I can answer *that*—and yet I never did but one criminal deed in my whole life, and I have done a great many so-called good ones to set over against it."

"Then you can answer neither question with a single word," I said. He took my hand and pressed it with the frenzy of a new hope.

"At least one man's philosophy is not all words," he said. "You act upon your theories. You are the only one I ever knew who did."

"Perhaps I am the only one you ever gave the chance," I replied, still holding his hand.

We stood thus silent for a moment, then he said with an inexpressible accent of satire: "Would you advise me to try it, doctor, with anyone else?" I deliberated some time before I replied. Then I said: "No, I am sorry to say that I fear it would not be safe. There is still so much tiger in the human race. No, do not tell your story again to any one; it can do no good. Most certainly I would advise you *not* to try it ever again."

As I left the room he said: "True, true. It can do no good, none whatever."

The next day he left. I never saw him again. Two years later I received a kind letter from him in which he greatly over-estimated all I had done for him. The letter came from St. Petersburg and was signed "T. Lathro Campbell, Col. Imperial Guard."

I fancied, in spite of his letter, that he would rather sever all connection with this country, and feel that he had no ties nor past; so I never answered his letter.

Sometimes I wonder if he misunderstood my silence, and accepted it as a token of unfriendliness—and yet—well, I have never been able to decide just what would be least painful to him; so I let it drift into years of silence, and perhaps, after all, these very good intentions of mine may be only cobble-stones added to the paving of the streets of a certain dread, but very populous city which is, in these days of agnosticism quite a matter of jest in polite society.

Who shall say? Which would he prefer, friendly communication or silence and forgetfulness?

THE END